Tears of a Gangsta 2

Lock Down Publications & Ca$h Presents
Tears of Gangsta 2
A Novel by *De'Kari*

Lock Down Publications

P.O. Box 944
Stockbridge, Ga 30281

Visit our website at www.lockdownpublications.com

Cover design and layout by: **Dynasty's Cover Me**
Book interior design by: **Shawn Walker**
Edited by: **Kiera Northington**

Stay Connected with Us!

Text **LOCKDOWN** to 22828 to stay up-to-date with new releases, sneak peaks, contests and more…
Or **CLICK HERE** to sign up.

Like our page on Facebook:

Lock Down Publications: Facebook

Join Lock Down Publications/The New Era Reading Group

Follow us on Instagram:

Lock Down Publications: Instagram

Email Us: We want to hear from you!

Submission Guideline

Submit the first three chapters of your completed manuscript to ldpsubmissions@gmail.com, subject line: Your book's title. The manuscript must be in a .doc file and sent as an attachment. Document should be in Times New Roman, double spaced and in size 12 font. Also, provide your synopsis and full contact information. If sending multiple submissions, they must each be in a separate email.

Have a story but no way to send it electronically? You can still submit to LDP/Ca$h Presents. Send in the first three chapters, written or typed, of your completed manuscript to:

LDP: Submissions Dept
P.O. Box 944
Stockbridge, Ga 30281

*DO NOT send original manuscript. Must be a duplicate. *

Provide your synopsis and a cover letter containing your full contact information.

Thanks for considering LDP and Ca$h Presents.

De'Kari

DEDICATION

This book is dedicated to the brothas and the struggle.
May God hear our plight and continue to give us the strength
to get through the night.
Long live the will to win!
One Aim - One Struggle - One Goal!

NEVA DIE!

THANKS AND GRATITUDE

From the bottom of my heart, I give you my deepest most sincere thanks, for never giving up, always supporting me and believing in me. Pushing me to fulfill my potential, never letting me settle for less. For loving me unconditionally, even when I wasn't loveable. Most importantly, I thank you for believing in me and standing tall right by my side as we go through Hell, facing the biggest fight of our lives. You ignored gossip, saw through the lies and didn't allow people's opinion of me to change yours. Thank you! It took the unbelievable for us to receive the unthinkable! God is good. Magik is real.

I'll see you soon!

De'Kari

CHAPTER 1

The first thing to hit me was the cool early morning air. It was just cold enough to get your attention, but not cold enough to freeze you to death.

I've always been a morning person, so I wasn't feeling all grumpy and tired like most of these tired, scared ass niggaz that were on the bus with me.

We were leaving the Deuel Vocational Institute in Tracy, California. Also known as DVI, or "Gladiator School,." which is a Level 3 penitentiary.

We were on our way to Pelican Bay State Prison, known as PBSP, in Northern California. Pelican Bay is one of the most gruesome Level 4 maximum security prisons in California. Let's just say this, it's a killing field!

Real talk!

Pelican Bay has the reputation of being California's most deadly prison. It's where all the bad asses Like Razor, Yogi, Mutiwalli and a bunch more were sent. Which is why most of these dudes on the bus with me are so shook. They are literally scared silent!

Not me, my name is La'Mont Simpson, aka Jason mothafuck'n Voorheeze. I arrived at DVI over two years ago with twelve points, a Level 1. Due to a juvenile escape, I was p-coded, which meant I couldn't go to any camps or ranches, like the rest of the Level 1's. I had to be behind the wall. Thus, I was sent to a Level 3 prison as an override. An O.G. told me they, the administration, was trying to teach me a lesson by sending me to Gladiator School.

Here we are, a year later. I am only nineteen. I have sixty-eight points, which made me a Level 4, and over five kills under my belt. And I was in the fast lane on the highway of making a name for myself in the largest, most dangerous, political organization in America.

I guess I taught them a lesson!

Now, I don't mean any disrespect. I know a lot of gang bangers out there just read that line and feel some kind of way about me saying, "the largest, most dangerous organization."

First, we have functioning chapters in over thirty-one states, functioning under more than twenty different banners. So yes, we are the largest. And as far as being the most dangerous. I'll just say this. Gangs have other rival gangs as enemies. Some of you are more deadly than us, as far as body counts go.

However, we have no other organizational enemy. Our enemy is the United States Government! Period! Point blank! We fight to overthrow the leaders of injustice and racial dictatorship masked as democracy.

We plan, plot and strategize and when we strike, it's with lethal precision. Our strategical alliance is why we have been feared so and labeled a domestic terrorist group long before 911. We are the largest analytical organizational body to challenge the government.

We are a threat to the establishment which makes us the most dangerous.

Now it should become clear to the readers why I am not grumpy nor scared. Hell, I'm on my way to becoming a legend, LMFAO.

The only thing I was not prepared for was the long ass bus ride we had to take in order to get there. I don't know how long it is naturally from Tracy to Pelican Bay, which is in Crescent City. I know it's nine hours from the Bay Area.

However, we stopped at several other prisons along the way, to drop people off and pick people up. Shit we didn't get to Crescent City for over fifteen hours.

All the punk-ass police gave us to eat were peanut butter and jelly choke sandwiches with nothing to wash the shit down. While they stopped at Wendy's and ate that shit in front of us.

Anyway, I swear by the fire that I breathe. The worst part, or scariest part of the trip, was driving up the cliffs to get to the prison.

It's a double-lane highway that runs along the north Pacific Ocean. The prison transport bus, which is nicknamed "The Grey Goose," is an actual charter bus, it barely fit in one lane.

At one point on the drive there was a mountain on the right side of the bus only inches away from the window. To the left, all I could see was an ocean, no road.

I had a window seat and made the mistake of looking down to see how much road we had. All the "gangsta" left out of me as all I saw was ocean.

I guess now would be a good time to mention I am afraid of heights. I kept seeing images of the bus going over the cliff. Me being thrown from the bus, sinking in leg irons and waist shackles, surrounded by great white sharks. How could I possibly remain in gangsta mode after having those visons.

The fact that I was aware of prison buses that have gone over the edge, as well as visitors traveling to see loved ones, didn't help me any.

Images of me drowning in the freezing ocean quickly left my mind the moment we pulled up to the prison gates.

"For all of you sons of bitches who think you're tough shit, take a good look at those words and pray you make it out of here alive," one of the transport officers, an Uncle Tom ass nigga said with a smile on his face. He was pointing at the prison gate. When I looked at it, I was staring at an eighteen-foot electric wall with razor and barb wire on top of it. Painted across the wall or gate, whatever you want to call it, were the words, No Warning Shots Fired!

They were painted in two rows in letters that had to be at least six feet tall each. It was a very real blood red color. The first row said, No Warning Shots, leaving the word Fired all by itself.

Now if that didn't get a niggaz attention, nothing would.

See, in Level 1, 2 and 3 prisons, the police have a block gun, as well as a standard Mini-14. They must use the block gun which shoot three-inch x two-inch wooden blocks, before using the Mini-14. In fact, they can only use the Mini-14 if they can clearly see a knife. Even then, they must fire a warning shot directly into the dirt, giving you one last opportunity to surrender.

On a Level 4, they're authorized to open fire with the Mini-14 at the first sight of violence. From the stories I've been told, the C.O.'s on the Level 4, or 4 yards as they're referred to, they don't even carry block guns. Honestly, I thought cats were putting the ten on the two with all the stories. I guess now I know they weren't.

For the most part Reception and Receiving, or R&R, at Pelican Bay was the same as every other prison. The police acted like they were hard as fuck. The thing that was different though was the noise level.

At every other prison I've been at, the C.O.'s try that scare tactic shit. They be yelling like drill sergeants in the Army.

Not here though. It was quiet as hell in R&R. All the C.O.'s looked like linebackers and defensive ends, with a calm assurance about themselves that let you know they weren't to be fucked with.

Did I mention, they were all white boys?

The other difference was, we didn't get any of our property. Instead, we were told we would get our property in about a month. Now that was some fucked-up shit. How could they really expect us to go a month without our hygiene, phone numbers and what not?

I wasn't about to cry or snivel, that wasn't gangsta shit!

By the time we were ready to go to our housing unit, I was so tired I was ready to sleep for two years.

We found out we would be on orientation for a month. Two weeks of which would be spent in building 6, which was the orientation building. I didn't give a shit. I was ready for some food and ready for bed.

We left Tracy at one-something in the morning. It was now after 3:00 p.m.

Walking across the yard to building 6, I couldn't help thinking, *So, this is the infamous Level 4, Pelican Bay A-yard.*

It was much smaller than I imagined it would be. There was a metal chain-link fence running down the center of the yard, cutting it in two.

On one side of the fence, brothas were playing a game of football and on the other side, were a couple of basketball courts, some picnic tables and workout stations.

Running parallel to the basketball courts were tables with stools attached to them. A small patch of dirt separated the tables from the basketball courts. There was a track around this section of the yard, circling some of the darkest green grass I'd ever seen. There were also small exercise pits along the outside of the track.

Overhead, the sky was cloudy, and the day was gloomy. It was nearly 4:00 p.m., yet it was so foggy I couldn't clearly make out the buildings on the other side of the yard. For some reason the atmosphere made me feel depressed. My mood changed just as fast as the overhead clouds rolled in off the Pacific. I didn't have time to reflect on my mood change. I was too busy attempting to take in my surroundings.

The building was a whitish gray-looking color, as if years of sea salt and sunshine had stripped it of its color.

Just then it hit me. That's what was wrong. It felt like I'd walked out of a colored movie set and walked straight onto a black and white set.

The only piece of color in this particular movie was the green grass. Other than that, everything else was some sort of shade between black and white. You knew what color they should be, but that's not what you saw.

Even the blue sky had surrendered itself over to the gloomy light and dark shades of gray. All fifty of them.

As I got closer to the buildings, I could faintly see a hue of what may have been red a long time ago. Sort of like when you could still see traces of a car's paint still on the primer.

All the paint had long ago faded off the basketball court and backboards. As was the same with the stone tables and the exercise stations. The steel bars were old and rusty. They looked dull and cold.

I felt like the prison itself was sucking the life right out of me and I'd just gotten there.

Finally, we made it to building 6. The big corn-fed white boy that escorted us sounded like Big Lurch from the *Addams Family* when he called for the guard in the tower to let us in.

Moments later, the steel door slid to its left, letting us into the building. We entered single file into a dark concrete corridor. I noticed a door immediately to my right when I entered the corridor. It too was made of steel.

The corridor was only twelve to fifteen feet long or so. The one door was all there was, until you reached the steel door at the other end of the corridor. It was already open, I'm assuming, by the same guard in the tower that was now above us.

Through the doors, we entered a U-shaped dayroom. The cells lined the wall directly across from us and flanked our sides to the right and left. At the time, I didn't count them. Later on, I would come to know there were twelve cells on the bottom tier and twelve on the top. Twenty-four cells all together.

For the second time in less than an hour, I realized the prison was much smaller than I had imagined. From all the stories I'd heard about the prison, I had an image in my head of what Pelican Bay would look like and this wasn't it.

There were only twelve of us that came to building 6. A couple went to the SHU and some went to B-yard. We were told before leaving R&R what cells we would be in and who our celly's would be. I was going in the cell with this O.G. cat.

The corn-fed white boy instructed us to take it to our cells, which we all were happy to comply. The C.O. in the tower told us to stand by outdoors and he would open them.

I was too tired for punk-ass power tripping games, but I did as I was told.

Once our cell door opened, I let my celly walk in first. He was an older cat from East Oakland.

"You can have the bottom, youngsta, I'm quite alright with the top." With that, he climbed up on to the top bunk without even making his bed and laid down.

Shit, I was glad he didn't want to talk. Although I made my bed up first, I followed pursuit and climbed into bed.

Fuck, I was tired!

**** N. D. ****

De'Kari

CHAPTER 2

I thought I felt like shit before I went to sleep. It didn't compare to how I felt when I woke up, which was only about twenty-something minutes later.

We had to be standing up with our back against the wall for count. The cells were your basic, twelve by eight feet. A steel bunk bed took up the back right-hand side of the cell, running parallel with the cell.

There was a two-foot walkway or gap, between the bunk beds and the steel footlockers and steel table that lined the left side of the cell.

My celly, O.G. Tone, had his back planted up against the wall at the back of the cell. I was in the front standing across from the steel toilet/sink combo.

Directly to my right was the door to the cell and the front wall, both made from... you guessed it, steel. The wall was six inches of thick concrete and the door was made of a one-inch thick sheet of steel that had a thousand, one-inch holes throughout it. This was so the C.O. in the guard tower that was approximately twenty-five to thirty feet across, could see clearly into the cells. If a cat thought he was going to get some privacy, he was on some serious drugs.

Pelican Bay was a fairly new prison, compared to joints like San Quentin and Tracy. They called these new prisons 180 designs, which basically were designed to eliminate blind spots. A blind spot was an area in the prison that wasn't visible to the C.O.'s. These were the spots throughout the prison where you could catch a mothafucka slipping and make him regret the day he committed whatever infraction that caused you to want to make his game up.

Most blind spots were nicknamed shit like Death Alley, Blood Corner, the Trauma Center, etc.

After count cleared, the tower C.O. rang the bell again to announce chow time, or what civilized people called dinner.

Five minutes later, our cell doors opened and like good little cattle or sheep, or some other form of livestock, we walked single-file towards the corridor. The door I'd seen when we first filed into the building was open. It led into a satellite kitchen.

It wasn't nothing like Tracy, where we were able to sit wherever we wanted to. We were instructed to fill the tables up, regardless of who the other three dudes were that were already seated. We had to take that next open seat. No questions asked.

The chow hall itself was relatively small, compared to San Quentin and Tracy. Instead of the fifty-plus tables I was used to seeing, there were only twelve.

I noticed a catwalk that ran the inner circumference of the chow hall, along the outer walls. More importantly, I noticed another big corn-fed white boy that stood on the catwalk, holding a Mini-14 like he was auditioning for a role in *Saving Private Ryan.*

Little did I know, the white boy would soon be taking his auditioning role very serious and very literal.

The dudes that served us our dinner trays, if you could call the shit dinner, all looked as if they'd died over a decade ago and gave up the will to live.

I was reminded of the old Wes Craven nightmare movies as I walked to the table that had the next available seat. It was just my luck to be seated at a table with three racist-looking-ass white boys.

As I approached, they looked up at me. The looks on their faces were priceless. They looked at me like they were devout Catholics and I was a whore of Babylon, who'd just gotten caught screwing the Pope.

They might've scared the average nigga with their looks, but they only managed to make me smile. White boys had the kid seriously fucked up!

Now, don't get me wrong. I never claimed to be the hardest, toughest mothafucka on the block. But trust me, I did my thang.

I sat down at the table and in my most white-washed, "Carlton from the *Fresh Prince of Bel Air* voice" said, "Say there, fellas, this here supper looks mighty delicious if I do say so myself."

They all turned a shade of red that was unnatural for a human being. They'd thought their looks would intimidate me. Little did they know, it's gonna take a whole lot more than three racist white boys screw facing me to scare me. Especially when I could clearly see the bitch in their eyes, they were all fighting so hard to conceal.

To add insult to injury, I smacked away loudly on the nasty ass food like it was 5-star cuisine and I was a child with no manners. I knew I was dumb ass out of pocket, but I didn't care.

Back in the cell, me and my celly were sharing a nice good laugh at the expense of the white boys.

Tone was a forty or forty-one-year-old, O.G. smoker (dope fiend). It's sad because he'd caught his third strike for stealing a pizza from downtown Palo Alto. They gave a nigga life in prison for being hungry. It doesn't really get too much more fucked up than that.

"Voorheeze, I'm just saying, lil brah. Did you see the looks on them mothafuckas' faces that were serving chow? Blood, they looked like zombies or some shit." I don't know why, but when he said this, Tone's mood went from laughing to sad.

Tone was like that though. One minute, he'd be laughing and telling a story and the next, he'd be on the verge of tears. I figured it had something to do with him just receiving life, so I didn't give him any shit behind it. Back then, I didn't know anything about people who were bipolar. Hell, I had never heard of the word then.

"Yeah, I peeped it too. Everything about this mothafuck'n joint is gloomy and depressing as fuck. The moment we walked through that big ass gate, I felt that shit," I responded.

"I know. It's like we walked right into a scary movie. You know, like in a scary movie when they come to a town and it's all haunted and shit?" He was looking down at his hands as he spoke.

"Tone, I'mma tell you what it is, Rogue. It's death. Maybe not death in the sense of niggaz dying left and right. But death in the sense that these niggaz done gave up on life. They done lost their fight, Tone. These niggaz' spirit is dead." He wasn't looking at me, so I made sure I got his attention before I finished.

"Brah, I don't know what it's like to wake up and realize I'm gone have to spend my life in this bitch. And a nigga ain't about to sit here and front about what I would and wouldn't do. But what I am gone tell you is no matter what, you can't give up like these niggaz. No matter what, you must always keep fighting."

"Shit, youngsta. Fuck you know about not giving up? It ain't shit to fight! I done let these mothafuckas give me life and now I gotta accept it." When he said this, he had actual tears running down his face.

I couldn't believe what I was hearing. Wasn't no sense telling him not to give up, shit, he done gave up already!

I wanted to try and get him to see he was wrong. There was always a reason to fight. There was never a reason to give

20

up. I couldn't understand how this O.G. nigga couldn't see the reality of shit.

I started to say something, but then I realized this was his reality. What the fuck could I say to that?

We were two niggaz stuck in two separate realities, forced to inhabit one confined space. This was our cell, but it was his house. I wasn't about to sit and let the nigga stay on some, "poor me" shit. That shit was contagious, and I wasn't trying to be on it.

Therefore, I changed the subject quick. I started talking about some street shit and before long Tone's mind was off the woes of his life. I had him back on the streets, his mind wrapping around the tale I was spinning about my street life.

About how before I'd gotten locked up, I was on my way to be the next Kenneth Supreme McGriff. He was eating up (believing) everything I was saying with a smile on his face like he was watching *New Jack City*.

Funny thing was, I was lying my ass off! But that's how it was in prison.

Either Tone couldn't tell I was lying, or he didn't give a fuck, he was just enjoying the story. Enjoying that small escape from reality. We spent the rest of that night, with me sharing stories about the life I'd wished for years I lived.

De'Kari

CHAPTER 3

We stayed in six building for two and a half weeks. It seemed like it was longer than that because we didn't have anything else to do except talk to each other.

Trading war stories and lies.

Then they moved us into four building which was set up just like six building was. We still didn't have our property or anything, and we were still on orientation for another two weeks.

At least now we were able to come out to the dayroom, each cell individually for a shower or a phone call. It looked like things were starting to look up for us. That was only an illusion though.

"Four building. Attention, four building, prepare for chow. Chow release in five minutes. Once again, prepare for chow. Chow release is in five minutes!" It was a female C.O. in the tower. She sounded hella good as she shouted the announcement, which could only mean she was fat and ugly.

"Well, Killah, let's go see what the 'Bay' has to offer us." Tone began calling me Killah after all the war stories or lies I made up and told him while we were in six building.

"This mothafucka ain't got shit to offer but illusioned opportunity, big brah." I knew he was referring to the niggaz in the building. In a way, so was I.

Tone looked at me like I was a monster with six heads, yet he was trying to figure out if what he was seeing was real.

"What the hell is illusioned opportunity?" he finally asked me.

I reached for my boots and started putting them on. When they racked (opened) the doors, you had to be ready.

"False opportunity, Rogue. Or better yet, the belief in false opportunity." Tone looked lost, so I tried again. "Brah, it's almost like believing a mirage or something that isn't real. The only thing we got to look forward to is making a name for ourselves to a bunch of mothafuckas that don't matter.

"Instead of being perceived a sucka, a square, or trying our hardest to make something out of this piece of shit experience we call life. We'd rather look tough and play gangsta so a bunch of niggaz would think we're hard and respect us. Rogue, if that ain't believing a mirage or a bunch of bullshit, I don't know what is."

"Nigga, if you feel that way, why are you always talking about and going out of your way to make a name for yourself?" That was probably the most sensible question he had asked me in the three weeks I've known him.

I knew he wouldn't understand the truth. I gave it to him anyway.

"Cause, I don't know no better." I stood up and stepped in front of the door.

Before he could respond, the door slid open. All he could do was think on that.

I stepped through the door the moment it opened.

When I stepped out the cell, I had my game face on. Philosophy and philosophical ideology went out the window.

It was game time, baby!

I stood in front of our cell because I knew Tone wasn't ready yet. "Safety and Security." If your celly wasn't ready, you stepped out of the cell and slid the door back, leaving it cracked. Then you posted up like the Secret Service. Nobody got past before your celly walked out. Not even his mama.

While I stood on security, or Usalama as we like to call it, my eyes roamed the dayroom taking every single detail in.

Usalama was Swahili for security. Our organization tends to use a lot of Swahili. It stems from when the old ones used to be in the hole (Ad-Seg). They needed a way to communicate without the police, the Aryan Brotherhood, or the Mexican Mafia being able to understand what they were talking about.

Though it began as a means of communication for the Black Guerilla Family, certain key words were picked up by the majority of all the Blacks.

Twenty-something years later, and nearly all Blacks still picked up on and used those same key words. Knowing the right things in prison, could save their lives.

"I'm ready, Killah," I heard Tone call out from behind me.

I stepped to my right to give him room to step out of the cell.

Once he closed the cell door, we headed down the stairs towards the chow hall.

At the bottom of the stairs, my gangsta senses started sounding all types of alarms.

I slowed down without breaking my stride and scanned the immediate area. Nobody posed a threat. Nothing seemed out of place.

As I began to cross the dayroom, the hairs on the back of my neck stood up.

Suddenly, I felt a lot of heat coming from my left. My head snapped in that direction.

An old white man was heading in my direction with the determined stare in his eyes. Ordinarily I would not have paid him much attention. I mean, for one he looked to be in his mid to late fifties. He was about five-six and couldn't weigh no more than a hundred and twenty pounds in full combat gear.

The thing is, he was gripping a "Lord Jesus" sword in his right hand. I mean, the blade had to be sixteen, seventeen inches. It wasn't normal to see something so big inside the penitentiary. Plus, he was walking with it like it was legal.

When you see something that deadly, it doesn't matter whose hand it's in. You give that mothafucka the respect it deserves.

I could feel the adrenaline surging through my veins like a potent drug, awakening me like ice was surging through my body.

I didn't know who this white man was, or why in the fuck he was on a direct collision course with me, hellbent on death. I did know things were not about to go down however the fuck he played it out in his mind.

I was about to fuck him up! Sword and all!

He was now almost ten feet away. I began to get in position to parry his first strike. Something was wrong. What was it?

I didn't have time to be second-guessing myself. Yet this was not the stage to be making mistakes on.

What was it?

Eight feet away!

"Fuck'em. Move!" My instincts screamed at me.

Then I saw it.

He was marching directly towards me, but his eyes were not looking at me. He had that far away store in his eyes like he was focused on something or somebody else.

If I was wrong and let my guard down, I was without a doubt, a dead man. At the same time, if I wasn't his intended target and I put him down, it would no doubt start a war.

Six feet!

The hairs on the back of my neck were still standing up. Still, I didn't feel like I was in danger.

Five feet!

Now was the time for me to strike. He still wasn't looking at me. Even if it was a play to throw me off, he would've looked by now.

I had too many years of combat experience not to listen to and trust my instincts. And they were telling me that I was not his intended target. I stood down.

Sure enough, the old man marched right by me. My eyes followed him as he passed by and time sped back up. A white boy who looked like he could've played Paul Bunyan was laughing with another white boy as they were walking without a care in the world.

The poor bastard never saw it coming. Two steps away from him, the old man switched the sword to his left hand.

"Get down! Everybody on the ground!" the C.O. in the tower yelled out, finally noticing what was about to happen, but she was too late!

When the old man hit Paul Bunyan, he screamed and howled out like a wounded animal. The impact of the large blade forced him to rise on his toes.

The old man whispered something to him before commencing to gut him like a fish.

Pa-Kaw!

The first shot from the Mini-14 took Paul Bunyan's pain away. She missed the old man and instead, blew the front of Paul Bunyan's face off.

The loud rifle shot echoed off the walls in the building.

Next, the alarms began sounding. None of it seemed to bother the old man. Not even the second shot that went whistling by his head, barely missing.

The third white boy, the one that was walking with Paul Bunyan took off. He ran into the closest empty cell with its door still open and locked himself inside.

I'd learned in Tracy a year and a half ago, you just didn't get down when they told you, even with real bullets flying. You could fuck around and become a victim that way.

First, you assessed the situation to see if it could possibly involve you or your people. Next, check your surroundings for any threats or signs of possible threats. Once you've analyzed everything and figured you were cool, then you got down.

Pa-Kaw!

Another shot rang out!

"Get the fuck down!" she shouted again.

I was just getting down when the doors of the rotunda opened, and what looked like the starting defensive line for the Green Bay Packers came storming in, looking like they were ready to kick ass and take names.

"Get down!"

"Get the fuck down on the ground." It seemed like they were all shouting involuntarily as they stormed in.

I could see everybody was down already. The old man was bent over Paul Bunyan's lifeless body, still stabbing the shit out if it. I thought I was going to witness the Green Bay Packers fuck the old man up. These were some monster-ass white boys.

They didn't breed white boys like these in the Bay Area. So, to me, I was looking at giants.

To my surprise, once they got about ten to twelve feet away from the old white man, they all stopped their charge.

"McMeally, drop the knife." Shit, a sixth grader would've ignored the request as passive as it sounded.

"Come on, McMeally, he's dead already for crying out loud. Drop the knife, buddy, and cuff up." That was the sergeant. He looked like Bluto from Popeye but sounded like a bitch.

For a minute, I thought the old man either didn't hear him or he was ignoring him too. Then he stopped stabbing the dead body and stood up. He looked like he'd just slaughtered an entire herd of cattle. Blood covered just about every inch of the front of his body.

He turned and looked at the group of C.O.'s surrounding him. They all took a step back. Maybe it was the crazed look in his eyes. Maybe it was the size of the knife, who knows.

After a few seconds, the old man smiled a toothless smile. "Son of a bitch won't bother nobody else."

He turned back to the body on the floor, spit on it, then dropped the knife and placed his hands behind his back. The sergeant looked to the C.O. standing on his left side and signaled for him to handcuff the old man. While they were cuffing him up and walking him out of the building, I was scanning the faces of everyone laying on the floor.

All the faces looked bored. Absent of any sort of excitement, as if this was an everyday occurrence.

"Attention in the building. When I give you the order, you are to get up and walk directly into the chow hall and go eat dinner. Do not go anywhere near the body on the floor, or the area of the incident. I repeat, you are to get up and head directly into the chow hall." I was so busy scanning the area, I hadn't seen a new C.O. walk into the tower.

Since it was a male's voice that came over the intercom, I knew they'd switched him with the no-aim-having female that killed Paul Bunyan. No doubt, she had to be debriefed and would be sent home on paid leave until the investigation was over.

The movement bell, which sounded like a high school lunch bell, rang.

"Alright, four building. Stand up and proceed directly to the chow hall. Do not go anywhere near the area of the incident," the C.O. in the tower called out, this time without the use of the intercom.

Five of the C.O.'s that resembled the Green Bay Packers stayed back, after the others had left. They were now standing by, watching all of us as we filed into the rotunda. Another C.O. was laying a sheet over Paul Bunyan's dead body. The white boy that hid inside a cell was trying to get let out.

**** N. D. ****

CHAPTER 4

The table in the chow hall was buzzing with conversation by the time I'd sat down. The C.O.'s hadn't bothered trying to separate the mainline from those of us on orientation. This allowed for all of us to become mixed up, while everyone else openly discussed what just popped off, giving their two cents in the form of opinions as to why the old man stabbed ole boy.

"I played my position. Sat and listened. No talk back," as Bay Area rapper Messy Marv would say. After all, no one ever learned a thing by talking. I've learned to listen.

In doing so, I was able to get the gist of what went down. It turned out the old man was some Scottish cat that didn't give a fuck about, nor did he adhere to, the racist politics of the California Prison System. Which meant he was the rarest thing on any prison yard. A white boy that wasn't a part of any prison gang or organization.

He'd been down for nearly twenty-six years and in that time, he'd accumulated nine confirmed kills. A confirmed kill, being a kill you were caught, re-charged and found guilty of.

This would explain why the C.O.'s behaved the way they did.

The thing about the old man's kills, they were all against members of the Aryan Brotherhood or Skinheads that thought they could dictate how the old man did his time. Either that, or some young punk, who foolishly thought he would make a name for himself by avenging one of his fallen comrades.

Apparently, the old man had been playing a game of chess with a brotha a little while back and the white boys wasn't feeling that.

To get their point across, they sent Paul Bunyan, who knocked out several of his teeth. Everyone expected Paul

Bunyan to die immediately. Four months later, nothing had happened.

Four months in prison is almost like a year on the street. Everyone began speculating that maybe the old man was tired of doing SHU time. The SHU, or Security Housing Unit, was the worst part of Ad-Seg there was.

Word is that the old man had almost eighteen years in inside of the SHU.

It turns out he was waiting for a visit with his daughter, whom he hadn't seen in almost ten years.

She'd come two days ago.

Although I was both amused and impressed by the story, I kept my mouth shut and my opinions to myself. After all, I didn't know the two mothafuckas who were at the table with Tone and me. Both of whom kept making glances my way like they were eager to learn how I felt.

One nigga was dumb enough to ask me what I thought.

I didn't even acknowledge him with eye contact. What for? We hadn't even introduced ourselves to each other, but he wanted me to gossip.

"Unlike the dead white boy, I learned to mind my own business a long time ago." I only paused eating long enough to say that. Then I went right back to eating, which was good because I'd barely had time to finish, before they began taking us out of the chow hall.

Back in the cell, Tone bust out laughing the moment the door closed and he jumped on his bunk.

"Damn, Killah! Did you see the look on that nigga'z face when you told him that shit?" He mimicked my voice and repeated, "Unlike the dead white boy, I learned to mind my business a long time ago."

He laughed so hard this time, he farted.

"Damn! Excuse me, Killah, but that shit was hilarious! That nigga looked at you like he wanted to kill you," Tone managed in between laughs.

I made sure to log that jewel he just dropped on me into my mental "Keep Watch" list.

"I mean, come on, Rogue. It's bad enough niggaz just wanna sit around and gossip. But Tone, the nigga didn't even know me. Nigga could've at least introduced himself. Ask a nigga's name or something!" For real. I didn't like gossiping ass niggaz.

My personal beliefs have always been, if people spent as much time focusing on their own shit as they spent worrying about somebody else shit, there would be less bullshit in the game and the world would be better off.

"See, that's what I mean, Killah. You can't be super serious all the damn time."

"For one thing, Big Homie, in case you ain't noticed. We ain't only on a Level 4 yard, but we're in 'The Bay'." This is how we referred to Pelican Bay, one of the worst killing fields in the state. Rogue, we can't afford not to be serious. Secondly, and I mean this Rogue, I've seen far too many goofy niggaz who died over silly shit, for me to be one of them." My mind briefly flashed back to my first night in J-Wing at DVI when the faggot nigga Dawoo had tried to rape me. With no weapon to defend myself against the faggot who was built like Lou Ferrigno, I barely managed to fight the pervert off me. The next day, it cost him his life when he tried a second time to take my cheeks (ass).

"With all the open homosexuals in prison, along with the undercover, in-the-closet faggots like Dex from East Palo Alto, who would've willingly given the nigga their cheeks, the stupid, sick mothafucka died trying take some shit."

"Killah? Killah, you hear me?" Tone snapped me out of my little trip down memory lane.

"Huh, my bad, Big Homie. What did you say?"

"I said, the entire world is a potential killing field. The only changeable variable is when niggaz decide to do the killing." Shit, I couldn't argue with that.

"Well, I'll make sure to wake you up if mothafuckas decide to do any more killing." Tone's new program was to immediately go to sleep right after chow, both breakfast and dinner. This gave me some time to write a few new verses.

I've been playing around with trying to rap for a little while, but once I met Dok Holiday, I tried to step my weight up and take rapping seriously. No lie, I really got bars with this rapping shit. When I get out, I'mma be on some real DMX shit. That nigga X is hard as fuck, but low-key, he's not fucking with me.

I remember I was working on my verse to a song Dok had written called, "Animal Instincts." The shit was H.A.M., hard as a mothafucka, when I went down memory lane. As soon as Dok had come up with a hook, I was in the lab writing.

It took me maybe ten minutes to write a verse that was so hard. I didn't even let Dok finish his verse before I had him stop to spit the hook and drop the beat so I could bless his ears. This was the hook he'd came up with.

"/We're animals out chere/Men eat men like cannibals out chere/ The strong kill the weak young Hannibal's out chere/ That's how we think you don't hunt you don't eat/ You need Animal Instincts." That was one of the hardest hooks I'd ever heard. It was only natural that I killed it.

"My DNA gone extract through these drastic measures/ My pack, we Silver Backs strapped, ready whenever/ I'mma throwback Cat Roc sweaters and T's/ with twin double-eyed Colt Dragons ready to breathe/ fuck enemies, my regime

handle they bizz/ I make a call stand tall, nigga firm in this shit/ I know dey hating cause dey fake, duplicat'n my shit/ Hand me down. Now how dat sound nigga, hand me ya bitch/ "Dey quick to flip whole fuck'n game turned snitch/ Dese laboratory androided niggaz claim dey pimps/ Mark hands with smit. I'mma marksman when I bus/ Deliberation over-rated opposition gets snuffed/ Depict'n a bluff with telepathic visions of blood/ Dese niggaz bitches and dey snitch'n, so I fill'em with slugs/ Nigga, ya knew what it was, Teflon, I rip holes/ a canal through yo neck and yo mouth ya brain ex-posed/."

I still remember how Dok shot my little verse down when he spit his. Initially, I was going to throw my verse away be-cause his was so raw. But, I knew my shit was hard too. Maybe not on a level with his, but it was up there. That was the first real verse I'd ever written.

Dok had been giving me pointers on my writing and trying to get me to see the benefits of us becoming rappers. We could use the money our music generated and our celebrity platform to build our dream, the Neva Die Organization!

We wanted to build an external branch of the Black Gue-rilla Family. A branch that still held dear to the ideology and original teachings of our forefathers.

We were socialists and activists for the people. A move-ment similar to the Black Panthers, only we were the soldiers and warriors behind the wall.

Once the CDC began giving the real fighting members un-determined SHU terms for being validated as members of the organization, it made way for all of those polluted with false ideology, gang-bangerism, and misguided concepts to rise as the new leaders.

These were the fake, drug addicted agents of provocateur who manipulated and misled so many. Dok, T'Rida, DeeDee, Lil Thomas, Lil Rel and me, we wanted to put an end to that.

In order to do that, we would first have to clean house and make a name for ourselves. We would have to make our targets fear and respect us. In other words, we had to put in work. Once we obtained the authority, we would still need money.

"Excuse me, brotha." When I looked up, there was an older brotha standing in front of the cell. He was looking away from the cell instead of inside of it. This was a sign of respect.

"What's going on, O.G.?" I asked as I stepped up to the bar. "Try to keep it low though, my celly sleeping."

"Oh, okay. Excuse me young Blood, my name's Mustafa. If you're brotha Voorheeze, I have a barura (note) for you," he told me, now looking me dead in my eyes. His hard gaze must certainly intimidate most.

I met his stare with one of my own. "I'm Voorheeze alright. I don't mean no disrespect to you O.G., but I tend not to accept gifts or kites from people I don't know."

Sure, Mustafa was a Swahili name. Them Kumi niggaz used Swahili names as well as some of the O.G. civilians. His name didn't mean shit to me.

"That's a good rule of thumb to follow young Blood. Yet I assure you, I'm not a stranger. We're kindred spirits." Then, he said something that only comrades knew.

Yet, I still wasn't going to fall for the banana in the tail pipe.

I hit him with a phrase to test him out. He responded correctly and then hit me back with a phrase of his own. Both letting me know he was used to the dance as well as feeling me out.

Given the clandestine level in the phrase he threw at me, I figured after answering him, there was no reason to continue feeling each other hat.

"Forgive me for the formalities, O.G., but I had to be sure. The barura, is it Moshi?" (Fire-but in the term I used it, he will know it's being used as hot.)

He looked at me and smiled. "Hapana! (no) we never pass anything Moshi in writing. That will always be zungumza (spoken). Unazungumza Kiswahili?" (Do you speak Swahili?) The look in his eye matched the smile on his face at my response.

"Hapa (here)," he told me as he stuck a rolled-up piece of paper through one of the holes in the cell door.

"Asante." (thank you)

"Karbu." (welcome). Though I was used to someone responding with sikitu, (you're welcome) I was versed enough in the language of Kiswahili to understand what he was saying.

Once he accomplished his task, I let O.G. go on about his business. Even though I believed Tone slept to mothafuck'n much, I still respected the fact that he was sleeping.

I didn't understand dudes that tried to sleep their time away. They needed to wake the fuck up and give the governor his time.

Habari, gani nduga? (Hello there, brother)

It's good to hear that you have finally arrived. I've been awaiting your arrival from the moment I learned you were up for transfer. Your orientation shall be up relatively soon, and I very much look forward to meeting you in person, as I've heard nothing but positive things about you. I was told by a good friend of the "Shoeless one" that no one knows you are in town. He wanted me to relay to you that he wants you to keep it that way. Once you get settled in, you and he will have

*the opportunity to sit and talk. In the meantime, should you
need anything, the brotha that delivered this would be more
than happy to assist you.*

Mojo Upendo (One Love)

Kifisi (The Hyena)

I read the note again, double checking to make sure I
wasn't missing any hidden codes. Over the years, some have
gotten so advanced in the art of espionage, they could hide
entire commands in one sentence.

How well you were able to hide a coded message relied on
the skill of whomever was decoding it. I mean, you don't want
to give a three-year graduate assignment to a freshman in high
school, do you?

I ripped the paper up and flushed it down the toilet, once I
was satisfied I hadn't missed anything.

A good friend of the "Shoeless One," no doubt was a ref-
erence to my birth father, "Barefoot Rudy." Which would
mean a friend of his could only be Zaidi.

I have so much respect and admiration for this man, I re-
fuse to say his entire name. I may not give a fuck about being
clandestine, but I always respect the clandestine activities of
others.

Especially the "Great Ones."

None of our comrades ever called George Jackson,
George. They always called him Little Dude. Hatari wasn't
called by his Swahili or government name. He was called Tiny
Africa. So-on and so-on.

"So, Killah, you're one of the Jama Boys, huh?" I hadn't
realized Tone had woke up.

"What, you one of them Jama Boys?" Even if the barura
didn't tell me that, Zaidi didn't want me to surface. Tone was
too unstable for me to be having him all up in my shit.

"Come on, Killah. I heard all that Swahili y'all was talking. Nigga, I told you, the O.G. ain't stupid. You know you're either Jama or Kumi!" He rolled over and looked at me like I was retarded.

"I don't know nothing 'bout none of that! All I know is deep East Menlo Park, 1300 block! You ain't been listening to nothing I've been telling you. I'm PLR, Rogue, Professional Low Rider. Nigga, make sure you get it right."

"Come on, Killah, then what was up with all that Swahili?"

"Whatever a nigga needs to know in order to survive, I'm gonna know. Rogue, it's called survival instincts. But look, fuck all that, Rogue. Check out this new verse I just finished."

It was easy to sidetrack Tone and get his mind off shit. I walked back over to the desk and picked up the piece of scratch paper that had verse three to "Animal Instincts" on it. Then, I gave Tone that lava.

"/Birthed by a hyena was raised by wolves/ Till I ran with and got trained by bulls/ if you fuck wit my team we gone act a donkey/ and we grippen on cannon wit Bananas like Monkeys/ I'm 40's wit a 30, dick 9's wit a 50-piece/ 50-caliber Desert Eagle spit'n Middle East/ survival of the fittest shit.

"Young Black and ignorant/ Me and my constituents moving like we militant/ But we on dat nigga shit! Godzilla's wit an attitude/ Dat anybody can get it shit like we escaped from the fucking zoo/ Yeah, I know we bonkers but you don't want no problems/ Bitch, you puma pussy cat like yo father/ 'V' I'mma animal, Young Black Hannibal/Bang neva die, spit fire wit a dragon though/"

From the way Tone responded, somebody would've sworn he was a youngsta. "Gaaawd damn! Killah! Woooh! Boy, I don't know why you're in prison. You belong in somebody's music video!"

"Cell 7, you are being too loud. Y'all need to calm down in there and keep the volume down." Now this old nigga done made the spot hot. Got the mothafucka in the tower on us and shit.

"Man, Killah, fuck that white boy. He just hat'n." Sometimes, I forgot Tone was an O.G.

"Yeah, I know. But I'm not tryna give these mothafuckas no reason to hold our shit any longer. Brah, I'm hungrier than a hostage." Hell, Tone wasn't trippin off his property, because he didn't have shit.

Me on the other hand, I had enough to feed a bunch of runaway slaves.

With that in mind, we decided to call it a night early. We had a long day ahead of us tomorrow anyway.

**** N. D. ****

CHAPTER 5

Like clockwork, I woke up at 5:00 a.m. in the morning. I took care of my morning business and was out of Tone's way by the time I'd gotten him up.

It didn't make any sense to me that he was never ready for chow. Because of him never being ready, I decided to get him up twenty minutes before chow.

By the time they opened the doors, we were both ready and on the move on time this morning.

My foot had just touched the ground when movement to my right caught my attention. Since it was toward the direction I needed go, I kept it pushing, but made sure to be on alert.

Cell 3 was the only cell remaining open. I was just getting ready to walk past the open door when my senses went off. I paused my step and squared up. Ready for whatever, except for what happened.

Something very large came flying out of the open cell. Initially, I though a mothafucka was rushing me. Then reality hit me.

I was witnessing a nigga tossing a dead body out of his cell. The body hit the ground with a hard thump like it was frozen. I'm guessing the nigga had been dead for a long time.

I looked around and noticed everybody kept going on about their business like nothing had happened. Like, I was in some type of time capsule and I was the only one witnessing this shit.

A little, Black stocky nigga, who looked to be just a couple of years older than me came out and closed his cell door, and walked to breakfast like it was normal morning.

"What's up, Blood?" he called out to me as he walked by. He didn't wait for a response and I didn't give him one.

I was beyond shocked, but I wasn't no dummy. I kept it moving and got the fuck out of there. One of the last places a mothafucka wanted to find himself in, was standing over a dead body. I don't give a fuck how long the mothafucka had been dead.

Since the corpse had landed, or more like skidded right in front of my feet, I had to literally step over it. I didn't let that shit stop me though.

Once I was a good distance away from the body, I looked to see where Tone was. He was right behind me with a look on his face that said, "Nigga, you better not stop! Hurry the fuck up and let's get out of here!"

At least I wasn't going crazy.

Somebody other than me had seen that shit go down. Now, I'd seen a lot of shit in my life, but I'd never seen somebody just throw a dead body right out their front door like some old mop water, and walk away like that shit was just normal as fuck! On top of that, he had the nerves to greet a nigga like we were neighbors on our way to work. "Where the fuck do they do that at?"

I have no idea what took the C.O. in the tower so long to spot the body. We were already seated in the chow hall and eating by the time the alarm sounded.

About five minutes later, they stormed the chow hall. Again, out of the almost forty dudes inside of the chow hall, a good twenty-five-plus went on about their business eating.

The C.O.'s made their way over to the table the Blood nigga was sitting at.

"Okay, Banks. You know the routine, let's go," I heard one of the C.O.'s call out.

Shit today was S.O.S. (shit on the shingle, aka biscuits and gravy.) I was one of the dudes paying attention to my meal and not to what was going on.

I believed biscuits and gravy was one of the best breakfasts ever created. One day, I was going to learn how to make it.

"McGriff, I don't disrespect you by interrupting your breakfast, Blood. So, why you tryna disrespect me, Blood?" Now that got my attention.

I was used to mothafuckas immediately complying to orders the C.O.'s gave them.

"Gawd dammit, Banks. Don't start this shit with me. It's too early in the fucking morning for this. Your celly is laid out in the dayroom, deader than dog shit. From the looks of him, it looks like you spent the entire night with him in the cell. Now, you know how this goes, Banks. I gotta take you to the hole. Don't give me a hard time, it's too early for this, Banks." C.O. McGriff looked like he was standing on the front porch of his mother-in-law's house, afraid to knock on the door.

The Blood nigga just sat there eating his food while they looked at him.

He shoved the last spoonful of biscuit into his mouth and looked at C.O. McGriff.

"You're right. McGriff, you've always been fair to the brothas. Come on, Blood, let's take care of this." The Blood cat stood up slowly and put his hands behind his back, allowing them to handcuff him.

I don't know why, but at that moment I noticed one of the brothas at the table I was sitting at wasn't eating his food.

"Say, Brah-Brah," I said, looking in his direction as I spoke to him. He was an older brotha, maybe in his thirties. when he looked at me, I spoke. "Brah, I don't mean no disrespect or nothing, but are you going to eat that?" I asked, looking at the tray of S.O.S. that sat in front of him getting cold.

He looked at the tray of food like it was the first time he'd noticed it.

"No disrespect taken, youngsta, you cool. I don't eat this bullshit. I only come to the chow hall to stretch my legs. You can have it, youngsta," he offered.

"Good looking out, O.G." I didn't waste any time switching my tray with his and going to work on it.

"Name's Blue Face, youngsta," he told me as I was breaking up the biscuit, mixing it in the gravy.

I looked up and responded, "Blue Face, huh? They call me Voorheeze, as in Jason Voorheeze."

"You mean, like the cat from *Friday the 13th*?" He asked the same question I always got from people when I told them my name.

"That's where it comes from."

He looked like he was about to say something but stopped. Then his attention went back to the Blood cat that was being escorted out.

Once the room was cleared of the escort team, the volume in the chow hall rose as some of the tables begun murmuring from conversation about what happened. Even Blue Face and the other O.G. offered their two cents.

I was shocked when Tone joined their convention, but I didn't say anything about it. I was focusing on finishing my second tray before it was time to go.

Back in the cell, I was good and full. Two helpings of biscuits and gravy had a nigga feeling good. If a nigga had two trays of any other meal, I would've split it with Tone. Not S.O.S., fuck that! And if he felt some kind of way, oh well. Shit! He'd get over it.

"Whatcha think, Killah? That's some pretty cold shit, to kill a nigga and then spend the whole night in the cell with the body. You think you're cold enough to do some shit like that, Killah?" I was laid up on my bunk, so I couldn't see the look on Tone's face when he asked me that. But it sounded like he had a smile on his face.

"Fuck, nah! I'm not about to sit in a mothafuck'n cell with no dead body all night! Rogue, that's some creepy ass shit!" Personally, the shit had me shook. I couldn't understand how a nigga could do some shit like that.

"Aw, come on, Killah! Now I know yo lil tough ass ain't scared of no dead body." Tone started laughing like he'd just told the funniest joke ever known to man.

"It ain't got shit to do with being scared. Nigga, that's just some creepy, sick ass shit." I was beginning to get upset. Only because there was some truth in Tone's statement. I would be shook if I was locked in a cell all night with a dead body.

"Again, like where the fuck do they do that at?"

"Okay, Killah! Calm down. You ain't gotta get all mad at the O.G."

Needless to say, the conversation ended right there. A little while later, Mustafa came through with a care package for me. Which was sort of like a, "here nigga, get on your feet" package.

The care package was right on time. It was full of some ZuZu's & Wham Wham's (snacks), hygiene, food, stationery and what-nots. But more importantly, it had a deck of pinochle cards inside of it.

Tone and I spent the rest of the day and all that night playing head-up pinochle. Maybe a better way to explain it is, I spent all day and night kicking Tone's dog ass in pinochle. It's a card game similar to spades. It's just more advanced and five times as much fun. The saying is, once you learn how to play pinochle you stop liking or even playing spades.

In spades, you have one deck of poker cards, minus the two of diamonds and two of hearts, fifty cards altogether. With pinochle, there are eighty cards. They're only the ace, king, queen, jack and ten of every suit. And it takes four regular poker decks to make up one pinochle deck.

The biggest difference would be in the game of spades. The spades suit is always trump, whereas in pinochle, the person who takes the bid can make any suit he wants trump.

**** N. D. ****

A few days later, I woke with a sense of dread over me. I'd only been at Pelican Bay a couple of weeks and already it felt like the worst place on earth.

Little did I know I hadn't seen anything yet. We were in the chow hall eating dinner. As usual, it was some bullshit. But I was starving, so I was knocking it down.

A commotion to my left drew my attention. When I looked in that direction, two brothas were going at it one on one. They were trading blow for blow, like two Titans in the middle of the chow hall.

I hadn't been paying attention to the two niggaz fighting no more than five or six seconds before I heard, "Aw, Cuz! That's the Homie!"

My head snapped to the right in time to see a big ole ugly, King Kong looking mothafucka jump up from the next table over.

I was guessing from his comment that one of the niggaz fighting was in the same gang as him and he was running to assist him. Unfortunately, I would never get the opportunity to find out if my assumption was correct or not.

Pa-Kaw!

The sound of the Mini-14 in the small chow hall was deafening!

Everything happened in ultra-slow motion. One second, King Kong was on his way to join the fight. The next second, his head exploded like a loaded piñata. He'd only taken two steps before his head burst.

Skull fragments and brain matter sprayed, raining down on top of me and the rest of the dudes seated at the table with me.

The shit had a weird funky odor to it.

King Kong's weight and momentum carried him another step or so, before his body dropped like a sack of potatoes.

I don't care who you are, or what you're going through. The sound of that Mini-14 got your attention!

Even the two cats who were fighting, stopped trading blows and stood looking dumfounded at King Kong's lifeless body with half of its head missing.

Naturally, the C.O.'s responded to the alarm. They stormed the chow hall like a bunch of Cobra Commander Storm Troopers.

I looked down at my tray. My runny eggs now had some clearish, gray-pink stuff on them. It didn't take a rocket scientist to determine what I was looking at.

My breakfast was ruined, right along with my appetite. I could hear chitter chatter coming from the surrounding tables. Still, I was oblivious to what was being said. My eyes were glued to the nigga'z brains on my plate.

"Breakfast is over! One by one, each table is to get up and walk back to your assigned cells," I heard the order, yet I couldn't determine which C.O. gave it.

When it came to my table. I did like everyone else, stood up and walked sort of aimlessly towards my cell. I hadn't seen him in front of me, but when I got to my cell, Tone was already inside.

I stepped inside of the cell and just stared into the mirror. However, I wasn't seeing my reflection looking back at me. Images of the things I'd witnessed over the past few weeks played like a movie, real graphically in my mind. I was watching these images.

The door to our cell closed. I felt something slowly sliding down the right side of my neck, so I reached my hand involuntarily towards my neck. My fingertips felt something gooey. When I looked at my fingers, I saw the same grayish/pink brain matter that ruined my breakfast.

Before I realized what I was doing, I was sliding down the wall of the cell into a sitting position. I landed with a thump.

I just sat there. I couldn't believe the shit I've witnessed since being here.

This mothafuck'n place was crazy! This was nothing like DVI. All sorts of thoughts ran through my mind.

For the first time since I was sent to prison. I wondered if I would make it home. I wondered if I could end up like the young nigga killed in his cell by his celly.

Or like the white boy who left his cell intending to go to chow but ended up in hell. Could I possibly one day come to one of my comrade's aid and die in the process, or as a result of my actions?

Killah? Killah, did you hear me?" Tone's voice sounded foreign in my ears.

In the fog I was in, his voice sound faint and distant.

"Huh?" I started coming out of the fog. "What you say?"

I was still sitting on the ground with my knees pulled up to my chest. I looked up in his direction. He was on the top bunk.

"I asked you if you were okay. Why are you on the floor like that? What's wrong?" I couldn't see the smirk on his face, but I could but could hear it in his voice.

"Rogue, I don't belong here. I don't know why these mothafuckas sent me here, but I don't belong here," I answered more to myself than to him, barely above a whisper.

A loud roar of laughter erupted out of Tone. He laughed like I'd just told the funniest joke man ever heard.

I was too discombobulated to be embarrassed!

We were doing our thang in DVI, knocking mothafuckas out and knocking mothafuckas' dicks in the dirt. (killing them) But we still were clandestine with it.

Sometimes it would take weeks to plan one hit. Because it wasn't just about the hit, it was about getting away with it.

Not here though.

It was as if no one gave a fuck about getting away with shit. Like, they wanted everyone to know what they did. This was some real, backwards *Twilight Zone* shit. They didn't have nothing to lose and shit to fear.

"I don't know why these mothafuckas sent me here! I don't belong here!" Tone mimicked me in between laughing. "Come on, Killah. I know a cold-hearted mothafucka like you ain't shocked behind a couple of convicts getting knocked off," he further taunted. I felt small and irrelevant.

I heard the words, but I wasn't stressing the BS Tone was spitting. This mothafucka already was serving life. So, I didn't expect him to understand the common sense behind me not wanting to get a case. It made me realize for the first time that making it home wasn't a guarantee.

I don't know how long I stayed in the position I was in, ignoring my celly's idiotic comments, and mentally coming up with a game plan that would help to ensure I made it back to the streets.

The C.O. in the tower brought me out of my state of shock.

"Simpson and Galloway, get ready for medical, an escort will be here soon to pick you up!" It was that sexy-sounding voice, belonging to the C.O. from the other day. I could tell that voice easily, due to its distinctive sexiness. I learned from

Mustafa that her name was Preston. I hadn't seen her face yet, but I knew she was beautiful, she had to be.

I was just finishing lacing up my boots when the door to our cell slid open. "Simpson and Galloway, let's go," the voice belonged to our escort.

From the distance we were, I couldn't tell if it was a man or a woman. The only two things I was sure of was, it was white and built like a grizzly bear. Turned out to be a woman. Biggest damn woman I'd ever seen. She was at least six-two and easily topping three hundred pounds on the scale. Her name tag read Finnegan. I figured she had to be Irish or something. Whatever she was, she was one big white bitch.

CHAPTER 6

On the way over to medical, I was shocked at the number of Blacks on the yard. Clearly, we were the dominant people here, outnumbering the whites at least six to one.

The irony of this is the fact that in the three weeks and some change I've been here, I have yet to see one Black face working here. Hell, I hadn't seen a Hispanic face either.

The medical visit was the normal initial physical you had to take when you first get to a prison.

The only exception was when the nurse told me there was a vaccination for hepatitis. I volunteered for the shot and waited for the nurse that would administer it to me.

I waited about fifteen minutes for the shock of a lifetime. The nurse that administered the vaccination was a buff-ass Black homosexual.

When I first saw his black skin, it felt good to see a brotha getting that legal money. The moment he spoke, I felt ashamed to be a black man. Not that I'm homophobic or anything, I was just disappointed at how we allow these white folks to play us. Here we had the "token nigga," but he was someone they could still laugh at behind his back.

I looked around, feeling self-conscious as he readied his equipment for the shot. It felt like every set of white eyes were looking at me. Mocking me.

I returned to my cell ashamed and embarrassed with very low spirits. Tone stayed in medical for one reason or another. It was cool with me because I wasn't in the mood for his dry-ass jokes.

I took advantage of Tone being out of the cell and got me a good workout in. I knocked out ten sets of forty-five. The ten sets gave a nigga a good workout.

Tone came walking into the building just as I was finishing washing up in the sink. I made sure to get out of his way when the door slid open, in case he had to use the toilet or sink. It was like an unwritten rule, if you were already in the cell when your celly came in, you got off the floor and out of his way to let him do whatever he needed to do. Which usually was using the toilet.

He came into the cell full of excitement. He took a piss first. As he was washing his hands, Tone finally let me in on why he was so excited.

"I just overheard the C.O.'s talking about us getting our property today."

Naturally, I became excited too! "Fa'sho, they need to run me my shit. Nigga, I'm tired of starving."

"Come on, Killah. You gotta stop all the charades. We both know you ain't got no commissary," Tone joked, trying to get one in on me on the sly.

"You can talk that shit if you want to, old man, fuck around and be starving in dis bitch. I told you, I don't do the fat mouthing. I'm telling you I'm sitting nice with the food." I had to correct Tone instantly.

"Oh yeah, I forgot you was balling out there, Killah. On your Felix Mitchell shit," Tone joked some more.

Before I had a chance to respond, the C.O. in the tower shouted out for everyone on orientation to get ready to go to R&R to pick up our property.

Shouts and cheers erupted along the entire top tier. Niggaz were excited to finally be receiving their shit.

Fifteen minutes later, we were in a holding cell in R&R, waiting for our property. The vibe in the holding cell was almost festive.

One by one, dudes were called to claim their stuff. Until finally, it was my turn.

When I walked up to the window, the white boy C.O. that was handing out property looked at me like I'd gotten his baby sister pregnant.

"State your name and C.D.C. number!" His voice had more attitude in it than the look on his face.

"La'Mont Simpson, P-54312," I responded flatly. Shit, I didn't need anything to get in the way of me getting to my food.

I wasn't ready for what he did next. He handed me a large plastic bag and literally opened all my Top Ramen Noodles and dumped them into the garbage bag. Over one hundred Top Ramen, all dumped together.

But if I thought that was crazy, it wasn't shit compared to the next thing he did.

When I transported my property to DVI, I had twelve jars of Folgers Crystal Coffee. This mothafucka handed me two small garbage bags, each with a large black clump in them.

I swear to God, it looked like he was handing me four kilos of Mexican tar heroin. These mothafuckas opened all my jars of coffee and dumped them into the bags.

They literally opened everything, except for the canned meat. They simply threw it away, along with any of our hygiene that wasn't in clear containers, or that they couldn't take out of containers.

I was too shocked to be pissed off. And too hungry to stress the weird shit.

It was only right that the first thing we did was cook something to eat. I can't lie though, it was weird grabbing all the ingredients from plastic bags, but a nigga did what he had to do.

Tone sat on his bunk the entire time I cooked, with a stupid look on his face. He really thought I was woof'n about having commissary. I was too gangsta to rub it in his face. Never once did I speak on it.

That night, Tone and I feasted like we were kings, on an oyster and sausage spread. It was a good thing I'd bought the pouch of oysters instead of the canned ones or we would've never gotten them.

We topped our meal off with a Copenhagen cigarette. Arnold Schwarzenegger's bitch ass banned smoking in prisons. So, you couldn't buy cigarettes.

**** N. D. ****

CHAPTER 7

The day we'd been waiting for finally came. The day we all came off orientation.

The air was filled with a mix of nervous and excited energy. Being off orientation meant we did everything that the general population did.

Mustafa came through after breakfast with a kisu, (knife) for me, along with the knowledge that we got stripped on the way to the yard.

I wasn't tripping, I'd already learned how to keister a kisu while I was in hole at DVI.

Not to try and play my celly, but he looked terrified. I could tell he was trying hard to conceal his fear, but it wasn't working.

I couldn't waste my time with him though. I had my own concerns.

By now, I'd bounced back from my little episode the week before, when they blew the nigga head off in the chow hall. I was ready to further my legacy and babysitting some old dope fiend wasn't in the cards. Tone was on his own.

I hung the courtesy sheet up like I was going to take a shit and keistered the kisu. It was about six inches long and made from hardened, melted plastic.

When I was done, I washed my hands and made a cup of coffee to take with me to the yard.

When they did release the yard, I was ready to go with my cup of coffee in my hand, and my homemade knife secure in my ass.

I made it through the strip-search area like I knew I would. The first thing I put back on after the search was my boots. If something were to kick off, I'd rather have my boots on and no pants, than to have my pants on with no boots.

I could tell the sun was out, but the clouds and the fog did a good job of hiding it.

Out of habit, I began to take a mental count of how many people were on the yard. Dividing the number up between the races, I counted a hundred and nineteen white boys, ninety-six South Sides (Sureño's), forty-six Northerners (Norteño's), and over two hundred and forty Blacks.

With numbers like those there was no reason to continue counting the brothas. If something was to pop off, we looked good.

I took a sip from my tumbler of coffee and continued to scan the yard. The brothas had the section of the yard right in front of our building. A basketball court and a walk path separated the table area from the buildings.

The Northerners were posted up around the tables next to the brothas. The Southerners were a ways down from them. And I could see the whites had the other side of the yard towards the end of the track.

"What's up, Rogue? You from PA?" I turned towards the voice, as a big ass yellow nigga was walking towards me. I didn't take him for a threat because he used the word Rogue, which was a word only niggaz from East Palo Alto and Menlo Park used. So, he had to be from the area.

Even still, I was ready.

"What's up, Rogue? I'm from Menlo," I responded.

"I'm Gus, Rogue, from the Mid," he told me, extending his arm for a handshake.

"I'm Jason Voorheeze, 1300 Sevier." I accepted the extended handshake.

"Yeah, I'd heard you had come on the last bus run. Your name's been ringing since you got here. Niggaz say you kicked up a lot of dust in Tracy." He sounded rather matter of fact-like, as he said this.

Gus was a golden yellow nigga. He stood about six foot three and had to be at least two hundred and sixty pounds, with a bald head. He had that pretty boy look, but his eyes told a different story.

"I don't know 'bout kicking up dust, Rogue. I've just been doing my time, you feel me?" I was shocked to hear my name was ringing like that. But I didn't know this nigga, so I wasn't about to run my mouth.

I decided to switch gears on him. "What's up with the layout of this yard?"

"Come on, let's hit a lap and I'll break it down for you."

I fell in line on Gus's left side and we walked the track. I listened as Gus put me up on everything that had gone on for the last six months.

While we walked and talked, he also confirmed my assessment of the yard by pointing out to me who posted up where.

They nicknamed the end of the track where the white boys were, "Dead Man Alley," because the area behind the baseball diamond was a blind spot. Not just from the gun towers, but also from the inmates. Blacks usually walked the track three at a time. I made a mental note of that and kept moving.

When I asked Gus about this, he told me they used the other side of the yard as a football field. We were not allowed over on that side of the field, unless a football game was being played.

Gus and I hit about five laps while we talked. When we finished, I had another perspective into how things were on the yard.

Turns out, me and Gus were the only ones on the yard from E.P.A., which really didn't matter to me. I really didn't care if I had homeboys on the yard or not. I was going to be straight regardless.

After walking laps with Gus, I decided to hang out at the basketball courts and watch the games.

After the first game, a couple of guys asked if I wanted to run a game on their team. I turned them down.

Let's just say I tend to get a little carried away with the trash talking whenever I play competitive sports. In prison, I had my share of fights behind my trash talking. I even caused one riot. Finally, I learned it was best for me not to play sports in prison.

I could feel someone staring at me. When I scanned the yard for the source of the feeling, I made eye contact with Mustafa. The eye contact was brief. I didn't know then what the feeling was about, but I registered it and stored it away.

During the remainder of yard, I spent my time moving around the area where the Blacks hung out, observing everyone. I would move from one table to another watching brothas either playing pinochle, chess, dominoes or poker. Although, I wasn't watching the games themselves. I was watching how everyone interacted with one another, as well as picking up on who was who.

All types of conversations happen over card games and dominoes. That was something I picked up on when I was still in San Quentin's Reception Center. As they played and talked, I listened. One of the things I quickly picked up on was the brothas in Pelican Bay talked a lot lower than the ones in San Quentin. More hush-hush.

No matter what, I couldn't shake the feeling of being watched. This time, I lowered my head slightly and cut my eyes to the right, which was the direction I felt the gaze coming from.

I knew I couldn't have been crazy, because the feeling was too strong. Still, I didn't see anybody watching me. That is until I stopped looking at the guys surrounding the tables and focused on the players.

His eyes were like something I'd never seen before. I was at least a good twelve feet away from his table. And even from that distance, his eyes were piercing deep into my soul. They were the keen and sharp eyes of one who was both wise and deadly.

I swear, they reminded me of a wolf's eyes. Although they were strong and intimidating, I noticed a trace of humor hidden beneath the surface of his eyes, surrounded by wisdom. I wanted to avert my eyes and look away. Yet, they kept me captive to their gaze.

Just when my intrigue got the best of me and I decided to walk toward the owner of those eyes. The bell sounded announcing the end of yard.

Immediately following the bell, the voice of one of the C.O.'s came over the loudspeaker. "Yard recall! All inmates take it back to their assigned housing unit."

I heard someone call my name, so I looked to my right. Gus was heading my way. I looked back towards the eyes, only to find an empty table.

He was going.

"Say, Rogue, I'mma holla at you tomorrow," he told me as we embraced in a one-armed gangsta hug. "Do you need anything? Any hygiene or shit?"

"Naaw, I'm good, Rogue," I told him just as we broke our embrace. "I'll catch you tomorrow. Good looking out on that though."

I left Gus and made my way back to the building. Inside the cell, Tone was full of smiles. When I asked him, what had him in such high spirits.

"Shit, Killah! The town is thick at this joint!" he said it like he was telling me he'd just found out he was going home.

"Why are you so juiced 'bout that shit?" It was a good thing for your people to be thick because it usually meant less people would try you or bother you.

But I'd never seen a nigga act like it was his birthday because his niggaz were deep.

All the stories that were told over the years about "The Bay," would make even the toughest nigga a bit weary. It was where they sent the worst of the worst. All the top shot-callers of California's most dangerous gangs were housed at Pelican Bay.

If the "P.A." Carr was deep on the yard, I still wouldn't be acting the way Tone was.

I guess the saying was true. "Different strokes for different folks."

"Shit, Killah, things are gonna be a lot easier with the town being so deep. Which means, time is gonna be smoother," he explained.

After washing my hands, I picked up a book by Louis L'Amour that I'd gotten from Mustafa and laid down to read. I could give two fucks about Oakland being deep on the yard. I was about to let my mind drift along the Western frontier. I loved to read because when I did, it took my mind away from prison. I guess you could say it was a form of release or my personal escape. Whatever book I was reading felt like I was watching it as a movie, and I was the star of that movie.

I left Tone alone with the Walkman someone had lent him, I'm guessing it was one of his "Oakland homeboys."

I tried to get into the shit kicker, which is what we call cowboy books or Westerners. For some reason, no matter how hard I tried to get into the book, the more my mind fought me.

I kept seeing the eyes of that old man. Those soul piercing eyes, that made me feel their power from such a distance.

The pupils were a goldish-black color, if a color such as that did exist. Staring into them was like gazing into nothingness, like a pool full of oil. I've heard of people using the term "Staring into a bottomless pit." I could only guess that is what they meant.

The funny thing is I wasn't scared, though I know eyes that powerful had to belong to someone very dangerous. They didn't bother me in that way. I was more intrigued than I was scared.

Just who in the hell was the old man? That was the million-dollar question. I had a hunch as to who he was. No matter what, I'd already made up my mind. I was going to find out.

**** N. D. ****

De'Kari

CHAPTER 8

That night, my nightmares returned. It had been a little over a week since I'd last had one. Still, it never failed, I could not go too long without having one.

When I was a kid, I used to get molested by my two older cousins, and one of my uncles. Shortly after the abuse began, I started pissing in the bed. It was due to recurring nightmares of the molestation.

Three things prevented me from ever saying anything. First, they constantly threatened me. They told me they would kill me and my little sister if I ever told. Second, I grew up in a house full of dope fiends who only cared about their next hit. Not one of them would give a fuck about me and what I was going through. Finally, I was ashamed.

Instead of my uncles and aunts trying to figure out why I just started pissing in bed in my sleep, they decided beating my ass was a better solution. Almost every night I peed in the bed and the next morning, I always got my ass beat.

I stopped pissing in bed by the time I turned eleven. Unfortunately, the nightmares have never stopped. They were always the same. I was a five-year-old little boy getting sexually molested by three people. The fucked-up thing was, I could never see the faces of my attackers, except when it was my perverted uncle. It would be years before I ever remembered who my attackers were.

That night in my cell in Pelican Bay, I woke up as I always did, drenched in sweat and mad at myself for ever allowing myself to be a victim.

Angrily, I lay on my bunk. Damp and cold from sweat, as silent tears of anger rolled down my face. At five and six years old, I was a scared, skinny, bighead little boy. By the age of nineteen, which I was in Pelican Bay, I was a two-hundred-and-fifty-pound nightmare.

The contract between the two were night and day, which made it that much more difficult to ever believe that at one point in my life I had been somebody's victim.

Naturally, I had an attitude that morning when we finally got up and walked to breakfast. Luckily, niggaz were very intuitive and gave me my space. For the most part, Tone had gotten used to my mornings of being quiet. He didn't know why every so often, I would wake up on the wrong side of the bed, as they say. But on those mornings, he stayed the fuck out of my way.

"It's not good to wear your emotions on your sleeve, young brotha. Someone could use that to their advantage, and it could prove to be a costly mistake."

"So, could walking up in a man deep in thought without announcing your approach," I shot back at the voice to my right.

"Judging by your hand moving to your jacket pocket at my approach, I'd say not only are you right, but my arrival didn't go unnoticed either." Something about the voice caused me to look in its direction.

After breakfast I had been so eager to get to the yard so I could find the eyes. When I got the card tables, I was disappointed to find he wasn't anywhere to be found.

Recognizing the eyes, I'd turned and come face-to-face with, I took my hand from around the kisu that was in my pocket.

A warm smile spread across my face and I slowly removed my hands from out of my pockets. I clasped them together in front of my pelvis like some of the monks do.

"Excuse me, O.G., from the stories I've heard about this place and what I've seen so far, I'd rather be safe than sorry.

Especially until I had the opportunity to discern if a person's an actual friend from a possible foe," I explained to the O.G.

I briefly caught a glimpse of a smile on his weather-worn face before it disappeared. "Believe me, my young brother, safety and security is always of the utmost importance. However, I encourage you to use more stealth in your movements."

His eyes quickly darted towards my jacket pockets, making sure I received his meaning.

"Good looking out, O.G... I'll make sure to work on that." This time I turned my head towards him to make sure I gave him eye contact. "Tell me though, who are you?"

This time, he chuckled. "Oh, I naturally assumed you would have guessed by now."

"I try not to make a habit of guessing." I did have an idea, but assuming is a good way to get yourself into a jam.

He was quiet for so long, I thought maybe he didn't hear me. Just when I began to speak again, he answered me and confirmed my suspicion.

"I am a friend of a friend who's known as the Shoeless One." He took his right arm from behind his back and extended it for a handshake. "My name is Zaiti. You can just call me Zai."

"Jason Voorheeze, Zai, it's nice to meet you." I clasped his hands and gave it a good shake.

The strength he shook my hand with was that of a twenty-five- or thirty-year-old bricklayer. Too strong for what I perceived to be an old man in his late forties or early fifties.

"Yes, Mr. Voorheeze. Quite an impression you left on some of brothas in Tracy."

"If you say so, Zai." I side-stepped the comment, a little embarrassed by the small compliment.

"Believe me, my young brotha, I speak with no wicked tongue. Take a walk with me, young brotha."

"No problem." He turned and began walking towards the track.

I turned and matched him in step, side by side. Stride for stride.

As we walked, I couldn't help but notice the stares we drew from people as we walked the track. Most of the cats that watched us, did so clandestine-like. But some cats just openly stared.

"There's no need to worry yourself with the looks." Zai's voice was just loud enough for me to hear him as he spoke. "Although we practice and maintain ourselves clandestine, everyone on the yard knows who I am. Believe me, all eyes follow me wherever I go," he stated.

This didn't make sense to me and I told him. "How could anyone know who you are, if you remain clandestine?"

"Rules of engagement, my brother. Always be aware of your surroundings and know who is around you. *The Art of War* tells us to know our enemy. They know us just as we know them," he spoke patiently. But I could hear a hint of humor in his voice.

I started to ask him a question, but before I did, he continued to speak.

"In case you didn't know, little brother, Pelican Bay is a prison designed to house the worst of the worst. Over time, it became a depot to house all known 'Shot Callers,' as well as suspected ones and the upper echelon of the prison and street gangs, along with the top captains of known organizations. As I'm sure you are aware. In prison someone is always watching no matter what. You can be as clandestine as you want but believe me, nothing goes unnoticed behind these walls.

"Most of us here in The Bay will never go home. A sad fact that we've all had to accept at some point. That's why it's important to us when brothers like you come here. They sent you here because you've caused so much ruckus that they hope you never make it home.

"What they didn't figure on was us that still fight for the cause, teaching you and molding you, instead of continuing to use you and risk your livelihood. In essence, they have given us one of the world's deadliest college campuses with hands on training and experience." He paused briefly looking up towards the sky. I guess while thinking of how to formulate what he would say next.

"This is why I don't want you to surface here. Even amongst our own, are those with hidden agendas. Not everyone who comes smiling and bearing gifts is a friend. Unfortunately, the Afisa (police) aren't the only people that don't want you to go home," he told me.

Never had I heard anyone speak the way he was speaking. The hidden truths about the devious underlined treachery within our own organization. I could detect the sincerity in his voice as he spoke of the many types of poisons that constantly attacked our people. The many faces of an unseen enemy.

"What good could I possibly be to the cause or the party if I don't surface?" As seasoned as I thought I was talking to Zai, it was revealing that I didn't know much of shit.

When we talk about surfacing, we are talking revealing yourself to the functioning cadre and letting everyone know that you are a member of the organization.

As we walked around the muddy track, Zai turned his head slightly in my direction, he had a look in his eyes that held many secrets.

"My brother, a silent guerilla is always more efficient and deadlier than a known or loud guerilla." I should have known from the smile that preceded that comment that he was indeed dropping jewels I wasn't yet ready for.

De'Kari

**** N. D. ****

CHAPTER 9

The more I thought about it, the more Zai's words sounded like D-High's to me. It was almost like I had transferred to a prison over one hundred miles away. But my teacher came right along with me. I swear, that's how much Zai reminded me of D-High.

Kifisi came through the other day and dropped me off a floater TV. It was a real, or should I say, much-needed blessing. I finally didn't have to worry about Tone. With the TV, he was happier than a punk homosexual with a bag of dicks.

Even as he brought me the TV, I couldn't help but to remember Zai's advice about people bearing gifts. I began looking at Kifisi in a different way from then on.

In the short amount of time we have had the TV, I have learned how to read just how deep Tone is into a program he is watching, by the sound of his breathing. The deep hypnotic rhythm of his breath let me know he was fully engrossed in whatever show he was watching. This meant I could do what I had to do without being bothered.

Zai told me word came from out of the SHU that Damu had to be killed. Damu was a cat from Compton who had been making a name for himself. In fact, at the age of twenty-two, he was the youngest "shot-caller" to ever run a gang at Pelican Bay.

Damu was the shot caller for the Bloods. He was a brazen nigga that didn't mind using muscle. The problem was, he used muscle one time when he should've used diplomacy. Damu took the line (taking over running the prison yard) from a nigga named Big Meech. When he took the line, the first thing Damu did was have Big Meech killed, along with his little brother, Mobulay. And that's what caused the problem.

Young Mobulay was a cat who was loved by all. A cat

everyone fucked with and respected. I personally never met the brother. All of this took place before I'd gotten to Pelican Bay, so I didn't feel one way or the other about it. I just know the brothers in the SHU, (The Central Committee,) decided it was time for Damu to go and unfortunately for him, I was the one that got his number.

It's weird how politics play out. This is what happened in a nutshell. The O.G. Bloods in the SHU wanted Damu killed, but they didn't want any Bloods to do it out of fear of a statewide civil war. After all, a lot of Bloods respected Damu and loved the fire in him.

So, they needed an outside source. This is where we came in, somebody knew somebody, who knew somebody. A favor for a favor was the decision.

And I was the answer!

While Tone sat on his bunk watching TV, I was putting the finishing touches on a new knife I'd just made. I still had the poker I'd gotten from Kifisi, but I'd gotten my hands on a straight-back razor blade, which came in handy for a nice slicer. Which is exactly what I'd made.

At yard, a small riot was supposed to kick off as a diversion. During the melee, I was supposed to kill Damu. Pretty simple!

Just as I was finishing up, Tone's program was coming to an end. I made sure to hurry up.

"Damn, Killah, why you so quiet down there today?" he asked me when the commercial came on.

Tone was one of them cats that had to look at you when he talked to you, just like me. So, I wasn't surprised when he popped his head over the side of the bunk.

"Come on, O.G., you know whenever I find me a good book, I'm going to dive into it." I tell him as I lay *True to The Game* by Teri Woods on my chest.

"You and them books. I could never understand how you would rather read than watch a good movie." He had the nerve to shake his head at me, like a teacher scolding a student.

"Building six, get ready for yard release. Yard release will be in ten minutes," the guard in the tower announced.

"Yard release, ten minutes. Get ready!"

"Tone, give me two minutes, big brah. I have to take a gangsta really quick."

"Damn, Killah! You take more shits than the law allows." Tone talked shit, but in truth, he didn't give a fuck.

He was content watching TV.

I went to the toilet and keistered my banger. I'd been doing it for so long now, it became second nature. Every day I hit the yard my banger hit the yard with me.

Tone was a cool celly, that's why we stayed celly's. He was the type of nigga that stayed out of the way. No matter how cool he was, I didn't tell him shit because he talked too much.

After washing my hands, like I really took a shit, I took the courtesy sheet down and started grabbing my gloves and the rest of the things I would need.

"Okay gentlemen, yard release, starting at cell one! Yard release starting at cell one!" As always, when the doors racked open, I stepped out in order to secure the cell and Tone. Even if I would be ready ten minutes before yard release, Tone would still take forever. That's just the way he was.

As I stood on the tier watching everybody, I made a point to look towards Damu's cell. He was in cell four, which was off to my right, down on the first tier.

It's not hard to miss Damu, at six foot two, two hundred fifty pounds, he was a little smaller than T'Rida. Only, Damu was three times as black, which is a lot because I'm Bernie Mac black. And he had long hair like most L.A. cats.

71

I didn't see his celly standing in front of the cell, but the cell door was cracked. This was typical for gang bangers. They weren't as security conscious as the rest of us. I wouldn't have been surprised if his celly was already on the yard. Didn't make any difference to me because the play was already set.

A couple of the brothas were already given the green light to kick off a small riot on the basketball courts. During the melee, I'm going to show Damu that I get it like Dracula.

I get it in Blood!

I couldn't really care less about his celly. If he got in the way, I'd deal with him too.

"God damn, Killah! You're not listening or something? I said I'm good man. Let's go to the yard." Finally hearing Tone, I stepped over to the side and gave him enough room to step out.

He was among the last ones to walk out.

When we got to the stairs, I realized I'd dropped one of my gloves. I told Tone I would catch him on the yard and jogged back to my cell.

"No running in the building!" This mothafucka in the tower never pays any attention to anything that happens, except niggaz running in the building.

I found my glove on the floor directly inside of my cell. Walking back towards the stairs, I noticed Damu walking out of his cell with his CL-20 headphones on his head. CL-20's were the loudest headphones they had available for us to buy.

As I walked back down the stairs, I looked up in the tower. The C.O. was busy watching what was going on in the yard, instead of paying attention to what was going on inside the building like he was supposed to. Instead of getting sidetracked wondering about what someone else was or wasn't doing, I took it for nothing and kept it moving.

Damu was a few steps ahead of me as I entered the

rotunda. It looked like he and I were the only ones left going to the yard. He was four or five steps to the door when a couple of white boys started fighting. The shit was crazy because you really didn't see white boys taking off on each other at Pelican Bay like they did at DVI. The police usually strip-searched us right outside about five or six feet away from the door leading to the rotunda. This is where the fight was happening.

Instantly, the alarm sounded and the steel door leading out to the yard began closing. Since the door was solid steel, there was no way to tell what was going on.

Damu just stood there in front, facing the door listening to and rapping along with DJ Quick's song, "Tonight." Our location would be considered one of the few blind spots at the prison. I glanced back to see if anyone else was around. It was just Damu and me.

At that moment, I could hear Ricky Lovett in my head telling me to, "*Never put off for tomorrow what you could do today.*" With that thought in mind, I kneeled like I was tying my shoes and pushed my knife out of my ass. I stood up and my heart was racing with adrenaline. Damu wasn't some sucker or slouch. The rumor mill said he had four bodies under his belt, (that's four confirmed kills).

I made sure to look up at the guard tower again before I stood up. Like a hungry lion, I stalked slowly towards my prey. My banger was clutched tightly in my left hand down by my side. I was three steps away from Damu and still he was facing away listening to the music.

Once I was two steps away from him, my arm came up. I had my banger lined up with his jugular.

I'd like to say I executed the hit with precision, but I didn't. I panicked and it cost me.

Damu spun around with a sinister look on his face, with a smile that said, "You know you fucked up, right?"

I had hit him before he spun around, but the knife landed off my marker. In response, he punched me in the jaw so hard that my knees buckled. He followed it up by taking a step towards me and swinging another haymaker. I managed to step inside of it and jab my knife directly into his armpit. In one fluid motion, I brought it out of his armpit and swung it under his chin. His eyes got big with surprise, which allowed me to go to work.

When I was done, I left him leaning up against the wall like he was still waiting for the door to open. Making sure to move as silently yet as swiftly as I could back to my cell. Before blasting Damu, I saw our cells were still opened, which meant the C.O. in the tower was still focusing on what was going on outside.

I made it back to my cell without the tower C.O. seeing me. Somehow, I managed not to get but a few drops of blood on my shirt. Nevertheless, I took my clothes off and threw them in the toilet with some industrial strength bleach. This was after I was successful at closing my cell door without the C.O. in the tower hearing it.

If anyone came in the building, I just looked like a nigga who was in his sweat shorts doing laundry. Once I was washing my clothes, the call to resume yard came. Not even a minute later, another alarm sounded.

They found Damu!

CHAPTER 10

"Come on, Simpson! Turn around put your hands behind your back and step to the bars!" The goon squad was at my cell.

Four of them stood there. Two of them had block guns pointed at me, while the other two simply waited for me to comply.

Once Damu was found, the shit sort of hit the fan. There were only six of us in the building and each one of us was escorted out one by one.

I followed their instructions and let them cuff me. They escorted me down the stairs and out to medical. As we crossed the yard, I made eye contact with Kifisi. His eyes were full of questions, but he wouldn't get answers from me.

I noticed a few dudes pointing my way and whispering. I knew those were the niggaz that fed the rumor mill.

"Suuwooop! Suuwoop!"

As I was nearly across the yard, the Blood call rang out. I never broke stride. I just pushed on. It was an intimidation move and I wasn't to be intimidated.

Inside the infirmary, I had to strip while a nurse inspected my body for any cuts or bruises. Next, I was escorted over to the B-yard. The B-yard housed the infamous SHU, the real "shot callers" and the mothafuckas who just wasn't listening, period!

They took me to a room that resembled one of those interview rooms the police put you in at the police station. For the next hour or so, I was interviewed by the sergeant and the captain of the goon squad. They asked me about seventy-five, maybe one hundred questions. The thing is, they asked them same questions about two, to three hundred different ways.

It didn't matter how they chose to ask their questions. My answers were always, "I don't know," or "I didn't see anything."

At one point in the interrogation, the sergeant lost his cool. He slammed his fist down hard on the table and yelled out, "God dammit! Simpson, you think you're so fucking smart, don't you? But I'll tell your little black ass this, we know all about your little fucking escapades in Tracy. And we know you're supposedly some hot new hit man for the BGF. Fuck the BGF!

"And fuck you too, you little prick. You're going down. This isn't gladiator school. This is the fucking big leagues. Keep fucking with me and I'll see to it that your black ass never makes it home!" He looked at me with so much hatred, a person would've thought I had gotten his daughter pregnant. "You better tell me something, mothafucka!"

I just sat and stared at the racist mothafucka for what had to be ten, maybe twenty seconds. Then I leaned forward and spoke. "Listen here, you racist fuck because I'll only say it once, so make sure you listen good. The problem with most of you stupid fucks is you're so midget-minded, you can't see the bigger picture.

"A hitman? You got me all wrong. I am a keeper of peace. Everyone wants peace, but not everyone knows the rules of engagement to maintain peace. You don't want to get dirty. That's why there are more soldiers than generals. Anyone can be led, but not everyone can be a leader. Sometimes, you must sacrifice the few in order to save the many. For example, let's say you heard someone killed a little twelve-year-old boy. You'd think that was monstrous." He nodded his head in agreement while looking at me like, duh!

"But see, you being a mental-midget, you would never know that if the little twelve-year-old had been killed, he wouldn't grow to become one of the world's most vicious and cruel dictators. You know him as Hitler." He was looking at me very dumbfounded by now, but the captain had a look of understanding on his face.

"What the fuck is that supposed to mean?" the sergeant asked no one in particular. The captain called for the goon squad C.O. outside the door and told him to take me back to my cell.

As I left out of the room, I heard the sergeant ask again, "What the fuck is that supposed to mean?"

"I think the young man just told us Owens was killed to prevent a war and considering the casualties we have when wars erupt, I say good riddance. The captain's words were cut off by the door closing behind me. I smiled to myself, knowing the captain would make sure that was as far as the investigation would go.

**** N. D. ****

Back in my cell, Tone's mouth was going ninety miles per hour. "I'm telling you, Killah, even before they brought you out in them handcuffs, I should have known it was you that got shit popping." He was filled with excitement.

"Tone, did you not see they brought out everybody that was in the building?" I'd been back in my cell now for at least over thirty minutes and he hadn't shut up yet."

I was well beyond becoming upset or irritated. I was pissed the fuck off.

"Yeah, but come on, killer, ain't none of them other dudes gone bust a grape in a food fight."

"Rogue, how many times I gotta tell about running your mouth about shit you don't know anything about? Nigga, you supposed to be an O.G., but you run around this mothafucka like one of these new booties!" I tore into his ass like he was prime rib.

"Aww, killer. I know you're not getting sensitive on me?" That was it!

I'd had enough of the bullshit. "Sensitive?" I immediately bolted off the toilet and got directly up in his face.

"Mothafucka! This shit, ain't no fucking game! A mothafucka just got bodied, nigga, and you sitting here talking about it like you talking about a stolen purse or some mothafuck'n bubble gum. Nigga, just because you got all day in this bitch and done gave up on your freedom, don't mean you about to fuck mine off!

"You think I'm gonna sit up in this mothafucka and catch all day, 'cause you running your mouth like shit is sweet or something?" My nostrils flared like a raging bull ready to charge.

He just stood there looking stupid. Fear seeped through his pours with his sweat. So, I lowered my voice and gritted my teeth, so my next words came out in sort of a growl. "If you really think I knocked Damu down, that should tell you that this shit with me ain't a game. Now Tone, I fucks with you for real. But believe me, I will knock your dick in the dirt and any other mothafucka's dick in the dirt before I allow any of you niggaz to get me a life sentence."

The bulge of his eyes told me he was crystal clear with his understanding of what I was telling him.

"M-m-my bad, Killah. I didn't mean anything by it."

Yeah, he was spooked. I wasn't trying to punk the O.G., but he had to understand he was playing with my life.

By now I had calmed down some. "Not only do the wall have ears, brah, but nigga… the entire front of the cell is open. Have you forgotten everyone on the tier can hear you because of all the holes in the door?" I was speaking in a normal tone by now. What I didn't need was someone hearing the shit Tone was talking and running with it. Not that I was spooked or anything. Because if it jumped off, it jumped off and I was rocking, period. I just wasn't ready for it to jump off over something stupid, like a nigga running his fucking mouth. Where the fuck they do that at?

"My bad, Killah, I forgot about that. It won't happen again." There was something about the look in his eyes, but I couldn't put my finger on it. I didn't push the issue any further.

"It's good, O.G. We all make mistakes. My bad for flashing and getting all up in your face and shit." I wasn't so gangsta that couldn't apologize to a nigga.

"It's cool, Killah. You good," Tone told me as he climbed up on his bed.

"Now, I got to get ready for bed." While Tone watched TV, I laid on my bunk and did some thinking.

I was reflecting on my interrogation with the "goon squad." The sergeant seemed like he really had it out for a brother.

Part of me knows I should've never said what I said, but sometimes a nigga just gets tired. I've pretty much always been a straightforward brother. Beating around the bush has never done anything but waste time.

Besides, even though he wasn't ready for it, I dropped a jewel on the sergeant that was priceless. If Damu hadn't died, there would've been a war fa'sho. There's no telling how many people would've died in the war. The rumor mill had been buzzing for some time. And the word was, Lil Blood from Bounty Hunters felt he was the rightful one to lead the Blood Nation. Considering Lil Blood had a vision of uniting all the Bloods nationwide, under one banner called the U.B.N. or "United Blood Nation," most of the older homies agreed Lil Blood should have the keys to the Carr instead of Damu.

I personally didn't give a fuck one way or the other regarding which one should rule over the Blood Carr. What mattered to me was the outcome.

I was tired of seeing unnecessary black on black crime. If a war broke out, although it would've been amongst only the Bloods, there would've been countless Blacks dying and I wasn't for that.

Don't get me wrong, I was and am ready to get off in somebody's shit if it's warranted. I'm just not for the senseless killing of my people.

As for dropping the jewel on the sergeant, it was simple, I don't lie to no man. Period! Now I wasn't about to confess my sins like he was the pope or whatever, but I wasn't going to lie like a coward either.

My reasons for that are simple. You only lie out of fear. And I, Jason Voorheeze, fear no man walking. Not to mention, I recite the lines of my oath every day as a reminder. And one of the lines clearly states, "Should I be slow to take a stand or show fear to any man, this oath will kill me."

I fear nothing but failure and no one, but the Lord God Almighty.

**** N. D. ****

After Damu's death, the tension on the yard was thicker than Adina Howard when she made the song "Freak in the Morning." But that shit wasn't nothing. It was always tension on the yard. A little bit more wasn't about to kill anybody. As I lay on my bunk smoking a cigarette, I didn't give a rat's ass about how any of these niggaz felt about the tension.

Zai and I have talked a few times since Damu. I was building so much love and respect for the old man that it was shocking me! I think part of the reason was his genuine sincerity. I'd learned in DVI that most of our comrades were either negative, conniving, misleading or just out for self.

I would come to learn many years later that most of the comrades whose fires went out, spent most of their time hiding on the yard, hoping not to get validated. It's a reason why brothas like Fati, Kijana or Mutiwalli spent over a decade in the SHU, while all those other Philistines walked the main line, pretending they were real. Nevertheless, it would be years before I learned this. But for now, I was an eager student soaking up as much wisdom as I could. Something else I would learn that would shock me, was how many states the organization was in.

If Zai's words were accurate, we were in over twenty-one different states nationwide. Zai told me about the brothers out in Chicago and I instantly couldn't wait to meet them.

"God dammit! Simpson, do you hear me?" C.O. Carson was standing in front of the cell. I couldn't believe I was so deep in thought that I hadn't heard him calling my name.

"Yeah, what's up, Carson?" I finally asked, getting up off my bunk and walking to the door.

"You've got mail. I've been standing here forever calling you." He looked genuinely pissed off. Yet all I could focus on was who had written me a letter.

It was from T'Rida's baby mama. For a moment, I became worried, hoping that nothing was wrong. She had no reason to write. That worry went away the moment I opened the envelope and pulled the letter out….

Voorheeze,

What's up with my little brother? After what feels like forever, this war is finally over for us. Or should I say, this battle? Because the war will never end. You only got a month and a half left. Lil bro, don't do anything stupid and turn a month and a half into anything longer than that. I am 145% serious about doing something with my life and being there for Moe and the kids. Not just being there for them, but making sure that mines don't want for anything, you feel me!

*I'll be touching down right after you, ready to do it mov-
ing. I'm talking ten toes deep, hitting the ground running. Niggaz ain't ready for what we're about to do. This Neva Die
family is about to be on some whole other shit!*

*Oh! I finally got in touch with Tae, aka "Lil Razor." He
still trying to call the movement R-Struggle. He fully behind
us though and is pushing hard in Santa Rita County Jail right
now. He must get used to the sound of Neva Die La Familia!*

*I'm just saying, V, I need you to feel me on something. I'm
spitting from my soul, so pay attention! V, I'm never going
back to prison, Blood! Never! I say going because mentally,
I've already left this shithole. Lil bro, I'm holding court in the
streets if shit gets ugly. I swear on the blood of my seeds, I'll
air this bitch out first. V, if we gonna be rocking with each
other how we planned, I figure it's only right to let you know
where I stand. V, you're my little brother and I love you! It's
all or nothing with me! I'mma get rich or fuck'n die trying.*

One Aim, One Goal, One Struggle

Neva Die!

T'Rida

Damn! I just sat there lost in my thoughts with a smile on
my face. I love the ring to his ending, One Aim, One Goal,
One Struggle! That was some real legit sounding shit. Leave
it up to T'Rida to come up with some shit like that.

I took another look at the letter. It was written almost three
and a half weeks ago. I guess that's how long it took him to
boomerang it from Monique.

Nevertheless, I was out of here in sixteen days and a wake-
up! Believe me, I wasn't broadcasting that shit though!

T'Rida didn't have to worry about me. I was a hundred and
ten percent with the movement and focused on getting my
money up anyway. Or like we say in the hood, "Getting my

weight up!"

Although I knew I needed to have a solid game plan for when I left, I first had to make sure I made it out of these walls.

"A nigga get a little letter, now all of a sudden he quieter than church-house mouse," Tone joked from the top bunk.

"I thought you were sleep up there," I replied. "Considering how that mothafucka was standing there calling me for so long and you didn't say nothing to a nigga."

"Shit, Killah, I was enjoying how pissed off that mothafucka was getting. I swear to God, Carson was redder than a pot full of boiling beets." Tone's laughter was sinister. I loved it!

I'd noticed that about a lot of the lifers I'd met. Their laugh seemed evil and sinister. Almost wicked. It's one of them things I can't explain. One of them things that you must experience in order to understand.

"Nigga, let me find out you tryna get me a 115, so I can stay here with you longer," I joked as I stood up.

Tone and Zai were the only dudes who knew my release date. I wasn't about to take the chance of letting the wrong nigga find out I was short to the house.

"Well shit, Killah. Since you already worked it out with your people for me to keep the TV once you leave, I can't wait for you to get the fuck out of here, so I can claim my prize." He started laughing so hard, he farted.

"Aw damn, Killah, my bad. I ain't tryna talk shit or nothing." We both bust out laughing.

After a few minutes of laughing, Tone looked at me seriously and said, "You are a good dude, man, and I don't want to see you come back to this mothafucka. I mean, look at me, I'm serving life for stealing a fucking pizza. A lot of brothas have thrown their lives away for stupid shit. Don't be like us, Killah. Be better and bigger than us. Walking out of here is a blessing. A lot of brothas will never have that opportunity, myself included. So, make your next move your best move and make every move count."

I was shocked completely. I've never heard Tone say anything serious. Normally, everything out of his mouth is a bunch of bullshit.

"Look at you! Suddenly, you wanna get all Fredrick Douglass on a nigga. Nah, for real though, O.G. I don't really have a plan. Don't get me wrong. I've been brainstorming on a few things but for the most part, I got to spend my time and energy focusing on staying out of the line of fire, so I can make it up out of this bitch," I replied honestly.

"Look here, youngsta, you don't have to worry about making it out of here. Trust me, you will. The brothers will see to it that you need to have yourself a game plan, so you don't come back. Believe me, Killah. The only ones who make it are the ones who plan." He sounded like he spoke from experience.

"O.G., have you ever heard the phrase, 'Don't worry about tomorrow, it will take care of itself?'" He didn't answer me. Instead, he just smiled so I continued. "Believe me, I know the importance of planning. I just understand that a nigga could plan forever for tomorrow, and fuck around and die today. Besides, what in the hell do you know about the brothers and what they will make sure of?"

This time, his smile got bigger and his eyes sparkled. I wasn't ready for what came out of his mouth next.

"If you don't remember nothing else in life, Killah, always remember this. It just may save your life one day." He lifted off his bunk, so he was sitting up straight and looking me directly into my eyes. "Nothing is ever what it seems, and you must always expect the unexpected."

"O.G., what the hell are you talking about?" I wasn't used to anything like this coming out of Tone's mouth. It was throwing me for a loop.

"Killah, when I was younger, I was just like you. Full of fire and testosterone eager to make a name for myself and willing to put it to work. I never once broke my stride nor faltered by any friend's side. My word never proved untrue, nor have I ever betrayed those chosen few. But what I did do was betray the one person I was supposed to protect and love, my girl. I put in work for the cause and I ended up stabbing my lady in the heart.

Every time I had to do some time, I accepted it, not realizing I was making her do the time with me without even asking her. As the years passed, my name grew and the fights with her grew as well. All she wanted was for me to be committed to her, but I couldn't because I was committed to the cause. I knew the war I was fighting had no ending, so I pushed on and so did she."

"Hold up. Hold up, O.G.! You're dropping too many jewels on a nigga right now. Where'd you hear those lines you're spitting at? You're saying some shit you shouldn't be knowing." I was confused and beginning to get pissed off.

"Read between the lines, Killah. I knew how many teeth a dragon had while you were still in school."

What the fuck was he talking about?

I knew God damn well as long as we've been celly's, this nigga wasn't trying to tell me he was family!

I decided to find out. "Tone, I know you're not trying to tell me your family."

"Shit, Killah, I'm not trying to tell you, I am telling you."

"Simpson, you have a medical appointment. Get ready, your escort will be here shortly!" the C.O. in the tower called out.

"Nah, we not done with this. As soon as I get back, you better believe I got some questions for you."

"That's just it, it's a little too late to be asking questions, Killah. Learn to scrutinize everything in the beginning. You won't always have a second chance to analyze a situation, and not correctly assessing a situation could one day cost you," he shot back at once, sounding more like Zai and Ricky Lovett than the Tone I thought I knew.

Before I could respond, the cell door racked open. "Let's go, Simpson!" the tower C.O. yelled out, as if the door opening wasn't enough of a clue that my escort was here.

"Don't be all discombobulated now, Killer. Go on and go to your appointment. We got plenty of time to rap once you get back." After those words, I left the cell shaking my head in disbelief.

First T'Rida, and now Tone. Both times, I had no idea someone close to me was a Gaitti. Both times, I felt I should have been able to pick up on something. With T'Rida, it was different because I hadn't seen him in a minute.

Tone was a whole other story. I'd lived in the cell more than sixteen hours of the day with him. You don't get to know a person more intimately in detail than that! So, how is it that I didn't see it?

Briefly, I thought back to the look I had seen in Tone's eyes when I was checking him about running his mouth about Damu. Now looking back at it, he was testing me.

When I got to medical and sat in the waiting area, I was still tripping off Tone. On my initial check-up, the doctor offered me a vaccination for hepatitis. The entire vaccination was issued in three separate shots. Today was scheduled to be my third and final shot.

About ten minutes after I was in medical, my homebody Johnny Blaze came walking into the waiting area. Johnny was a Norteño from the east side of San Jose and on the lowkey, Johnny was one of them boys. I'd light-weight been making moves with Johnny on the hustling tip. Messing with Johnny, I'd even managed to stack a couple of dollars. He claimed he liked my style and even went as far as to say he would mess with me on the streets. But to me, jailhouse talk was just that, jailhouse talk.

I don't know what was going on with medical today, but ten minutes later, Johnny and I was still kicking it and I hadn't been called yet. Right then, about four or five South Siders came walking into the waiting area. They came walking in like they were hella hard. A clear sign that they were on some bull-shit.

Johnny and I made eye contact and smiled at each other. A clear sign neither one of us was tripping. It was whatever! When it came to the whites or the South Siders, tension was always in the air and we were always on point.

That's when the medics finally decided to call me in.

Fuck subliminal and head shakes, I flat out asked Johnny if he was going to be cool. Because if he wasn't feeling it, we could get out of that bitch together or tear it up together.

Johnny was a little gangsta, so it wasn't any surprise when he told me he was cool. Reluctantly, I left him and went to see the doctor.

Inside the office, the doctor wanted to tell me about all kinds of preventative measures for a lot of STD's and a bunch of other bullshit I wasn't trying to hear. My mind kept telling me I'd fucked up by leaving Johnny. So, I told the doctor to just give me my shot and let me be on my way, which he did with no problem.

The entire time, that nagging feeling that I'd made a mistake wouldn't leave me.

As I approached the corner leading to the waiting area, I could make out the distinct sounds of shoes and boots scuffling over the floor, confirming my intuition I fucked up!

Immediately, I rushed to the holding cell which was the waiting area. Sure enough, the South Siders were going in on Johnny. Johnny was down on one knee, attempting to block blows, while desperately trying to defend himself at the same time.

The first South Sider was clueless as to what hit him, as my left haymaker connected to the soft spot just below the back of his earlobe. He dropped instantly.

The guy to the right of him, noticed him fall and looked to see why he fell. When he saw me, his eyes got as big as saucers.

I didn't hesitate to give him a two-piece, which I followed up with an uppercut. Two things happened because of the uppercut. First, the distraction gave Johnny time to get up. Secondly, the dude I hit with an uppercut dropped a knife.

Seeing the knife, I went berserk!

When the smoke cleared and the dust settled, I realized my count was off. There'd been six of them. Three were knocked out cold, two were licking their wounds and one was getting the living shit stomped out of him!

They threw us in the hole. I never knew they had a separate hole from the SHU. They did, and this is where we all ended up.

Fuck it! It is what it is!

**** N. D. ****

CHAPTER 11

I have mentioned my books are truth told through fiction. I have put a lot of shit on the table some would say I should have left unsaid.

If you've read my *Gorillaz in the Bay* series, then you know that T'Rida is dead. The faggot ass police stole my brotha, which set off a domino effect of shit. I won't get into that. If you haven't read the series, you'll have to read it to understand, feel me!

I say all of this because the weeks I spent in the hole I met some brothers whom I can't tell you about. And since shit jumped off that I can't speak on, not because I'm scared, but because I'm not into incriminating other people or dry snitching on niggaz, I ended up paroling from the hole.

Yeah, I spent my last few weeks back there with Johnny. The kid was crazy funny, which made the time go by. We ended up getting 115 write-ups for participating in a riot. I didn't trip though. They probably would've killed Johnny if I hadn't helped. So, it's good.

Plus, I ended up filing an Emergency Restoration of Forfeited Credits, since I was under a month to the house. It was my only write-up at Pelican Bay, so my restoration was granted. My parole date went back to the normal date.

Johnny kept insisting that he owed me for saving his life. Time and time again, I told him I did what I was supposed to. It was nothing. But he wouldn't hear it. He swore on the Virgin Mary, his baby sister, his hood and gang, and a bunch of other shit that he really was the man out in the streets.

He told me all I had to do was hit him up and I would be set. Finally, just to get him to shut the fuck up about it, I took his number and told him I would hit him up when we get out.

He paroled eleven days after we got in the hole. When he left, I used the time to think of a lot of things Tone taught me, one of the most valuable lessons I learned in prison.

As a part of my safety and security, I vow to never take anybody or anything at face value. I will always look below the surface and see what's hidden.

I had to get out and put it together. Which is exactly what I plan on doing.

"Simpson. Are you ready to go?" For the first time since being there, I saw a Black woman. I had to admit, she was bad as fuck! But I didn't have time to sweat a chick, sister or not.

It was time to go home!

"Yes, Miss Jones, you know I'm ready." The five foot four, honey brown cutie, with the short Jada Pinkett hairdo, had some "Lord Jesus" breasts. Reading her name tag was my excuse to stare at them bad boys.

When she opened the door, my heart started racing. I couldn't believe I was really going home. I slowly stepped out of the cell.

If I thought her titties would stop traffic, I swear to God, her ass was illegal in twenty-two states. I'm talking forty-eight to fifty inches easily, no exaggeration! The only person I knew with a bigger ass than her was Lisa, the love of my life. The woman of my dreams. Lisa has got to be working with at least fifty-six inches solid!

I got my mind off Lisa and focused back on Miss Jones and all that wobble-de-wobble she had back there.

We stopped at the twenty-foot gate with the words, "No Warning Shots Fired," written in ten-foot red letters on it. She turned around to say something to me and caught me looking at her ass.

"Simpson, I read your C-file before coming to get you. I would've thought you were different than the average guy in here, who looked at a woman and only saw a piece of meat." She said it with so much attitude, I thought I must've missed something.

"See, that was your first mistake, assuming. There's no thinking about it, I'm nothing like anyone behind these walls and far from most free in civilization. When I first laid eyes on you, I saw every positive thing I could see without getting to know you personally. Addressing me as Simpson, instead of Inmate Simpson, tells me you don't take your job personally and don't see us as animals just because we are in here, like most do. It also tells me you were brought up with good manners installed in you.

"Your short hair and no makeup tell me that you are aware of your natural beauty and are good with it. Reading my C-file before coming to get me, tells me you are efficient in everything you do and just working here itself tells me how intelligent you are. And you're a fighter, because you are a beautiful and short Black woman, inside a predominantly white male gargantuan occupation. One that is little accepting of female C.O.'s, as long as they are white and look like the starting defensive line for the Baltimore Ravens." Her eyes were as big as silver dollars and her jaw was on the floor.

Understand, Jason Voorheeze is a real nigga. So, I had to let her know the truth. "As far as looking at your body, let's keep this shit all the way real. You shower and lotion your body every day, so you understand God hooked you up with the perfection every sane man fantasizes about. All the while praying to that same God to at least let him see such a perfect body in real life once. So, hell yeah, I was looking! I ain't going to lie but I wasn't just looking. I was wishing that instead of this prison, I ran into you at whatever gym you went to, so I could step up to you and tell you my mama taught me how to appreciate a blessing."

God damn! I spit that shit! The look on her face said it all. She tried to recover and speak but stumbled over her words. At that moment, the tower C.O. decided to finally open the gate. This gave C.O. Jones enough time to think of an adequate response.

"So, you think you read me pretty accurately with your little silver tongue?" I swear, she was blushing like Janet on *Poetic Justice*, when 2Pac was at her with those verbalisms.

"I don't know about a silver tongue, but I would like to think my tongue wins gold medals in every event. Now, if I was wrong in my assessment, you would have corrected me, Miss Jones. I know you're Michael Jackson bad. And if you had a good man, you wouldn't even be entertaining this conversation. I'm a twenty-year-old convict paroling from a three-year bid. I'm starting over with nothing but my gate money. So I'mma hit the ground with both feet running.

"I meant everything I said and more. But let's keep it a hundred, even if you entertained the thought of giving me some play, all I have to offer you is a golden tongue and a ten-inch dick that's been parked in the garage for three years. And no, I'm not being disrespectful, just being honest." Shit, I was paroling and they couldn't do shit to me, so I spit my shot.

"Well, don't be too honest, I'm still a C.O." The way she said it sounded like she didn't want to say that at all.

"I think a woman with authority is sexy as fuck."

"Boy, shut up and let's go!" She began walking faster which only made her ass cheeks jump even harder, like they were angry. When we got to Receiving and Release, there was only one C.O. inside, a white homosexual who tried to hide it but couldn't. I got my dress-outs that Nicole sent me and walked to the holding cell in the back to change. I could hear the two of them whispering and snickering as I made my way down the hall, but I paid it no mind.

I inspected my dress-outs before getting undressed. I had a black and charcoal Kenneth Cole jumpsuit, with a pair of black Kenneth Cole sandals. Oh yeah, a fresh white T, a white wife beater and some black Kenneth Cole boxer briefs. Shit, I was gone be on point!

I stripped down out of my prison clothes and underwear. Just as I was taking the boxers from around my second leg, the bars opened.

"Hmmh, it doesn't look ten inches to me." C.O. Jones came walking into the holding cell.

"I ain't worried about it. Believe me, that thang go Go-Go Gadget when he supposed to. But what you back here for? If you felt disrespected by my bluntness, forgive me. But you know ole boy is up there, and I'm not trying to catch a case." I was completely butt naked, so this could be bad. Just the thought of getting a chance to explore her body woke my little man up.

Her response was to unzip her jumpsuit and step out of it. Dear God, I was fucked. All she had on was her tight bra and panties. I couldn't help myself. My dick rocked up. Even if I fantasized about her one hundred times, I would've never guessed fully just how breathtaking her body was. Breasts that huge wasn't supposed to stand up. They were at least 44-DD's.

She stepped directly up to me, licking her lips.

"Don't worry about Hedgecock. He has two boy toy's here, and I keep watch while he plays with them. He owes me, and mama is collecting," she whispered in my ear.

She licked the lobe and wrapped her hand around my full ten inches. "Mmmm, I see you weren't telling lies. The van leaves to drive you to the Greyhound in two and a half hours. Show me what a man does with such a masterpiece of perfection," she purred in my ear as her hand gently began stroking me.

My hand immediately went to her ass. I had to caress it first. I always believed if you were in for a penny, then you were in for a dollar. Therefore, I said fuck it! I'd give her one hell of a memory.

While my hands were rubbing that ass, she was staring me directly in the eyes as she continued to stroke me. My tongue teasingly traced her lips.

I could see the hunger in her eyes, the moment I said fuck it. I reached up swiftly and tore her bra off her like it was made from tissue paper. One hand went back to her ass cheeks, while the other found a breast and rubbed her bullet-size nipple. At the same time, my mouth and tongue finally invaded her hot wet, sweet mouth.

We passionately kissed and fondled each other for a couple of minutes, I broke the kiss with intentions of sucking on her breast. She had different plans. She took a step back and dropped down to her knees. Shy was not a word that would describe C.O. Jones. She tried to take all of me into her mouth, only stopping when she couldn't contain her gag reflex any longer.

After her deep throat attempt, she went to work, sucking and slurping passionately like my shit was a popsicle. She was using so much spit, it was overflowing and running down her chin. Shit was crazy, especially when she started stroking while she sucked. I had to stop her before I came.

All of a sudden, she produced a Magnum condom and tried to hand it to me. I don't know where she got it from, but I refused to grab the condom, making her put it on.

I stepped back and reached down to help her up. She had a look in her eyes as if she was possessed, and a devilish grin on her face. I guided her to one of the wooden benches and sat down, motioning for her to climb up on top.

She eased down deliciously slow. Just when I thought shit couldn't get any better, I felt the tightness of her pussy surrounding and suffocating me. Even with her fluids rushing down my shaft, the tightness was still unbelievable.

Once she slid all the way down, she stayed there for a while grinding in small circles. I acted as if her bullet-size nipples were candy gum drops. I sucked a bit, tasting the real candy. Finally, she began lifting to my rhythm. Her ass cheeks were clapping thunderously against each other.

"Oooh, fuck! This is exactly what I've been waiting on. Grab my ass cheeks." She was yelling like we were at a motel, instead of a prison.

I didn't need much encouragement, complying to her request. I grabbed both of her cheeks and took over the show. I was forcing her up and down as hard and fast as I could, while thrusting upwards just as hard.

"Yes! Oh, fuck yes, yes! Fuck me, Simpson! Fuck me!" She had her head tilted back with her eyes closed. While I sucked one tit, the other kept slapping against my face.

"Man, I feel it! Harder Simpson, harder," she pleaded.

I was done playing games. I put my arms under her legs and cupped her ass. Then I stood up. She knew what was coming. Holding her up in the air, I fucked her like I was mad at her. I've never felt so much fluid raining over my shaft. The shit was beyond beautiful. It was amazing! Heavenly!

When she came, she bit down on my right trapezoid muscle. The whole time she growled, "Fuck yeah! Fuck yeah. Fuck yeah!"

I waited for all her aftershocks to subside before I let her down and bent her over the sink-toilet combo. When I slid inside of her, she came again. I grabbed her cheeks again and fucked like a porn star. She started throwing it back at me and my knees buckled. "Can you handle all this ass, Simpson?" She was smiling when she asked. Teasing me, challenging me.

"Shut the fuck up and take this dick!" I growled.

"Ooooh! You think you in charge. Then give it to me. Talk that shit!" she challenged. I accepted! I leaned forward and wrapped my arm around her throat. Then I choked her and fucked her until she gushed all over the place. It was like a water hose spraying!

She soaked us, the bench and the floor.

We ended up fucking two more times before it was all said and done. Every time I released it was on her ass.

Before I left, C.O. Jones slid me her number. I told her I would for sure reach out to her in a few days to see what was good.

It took almost an hour and a half for my bus to arrive. That was cool with me. I passed the time replaying what just took place with C.O. Jones. That was for real, for real some *Zane's Sex Chronicles* shit!

I enjoyed every minute of the twelve and a half hours it took for us to finally make it to the West Oakland Greyhound station. It was May 13 and the clear blue sky was the first sign of summer. The cool light breeze that blew made the bright shining sun feel like it was kissing on a nigga'z skin.

By the time I walked out of the station, the sun was getting ready to start its descent. The streets were filthy, and the air was acrid, but I took a deep breath and smiled. I'd take the polluted aroma of West Oakland, over the smell behind prison walls any day.

At first, I was going to call Nicole, after all she did send a nigga his dress-outs. But I called my "Sugar Walls" from the pay phone. She made it from East Oakland around twenty minutes later.

**** N. D. ****

De'Kari

CHAPTER 12

I wish I could say I got my money up and the rest was history, but it didn't go down like that. A week after coming home, I was MC Hammer broke, hungry, and starting to feel bad for myself on some "poor me" shit.

I'd spent one hundred and eighty dollars on the Greyhound ticket. My little Sugar Walls would buy me whatever I needed but wouldn't give me one red cent! Talking about what she didn't believe in that and shit.

Bitch, I don't believe in sitting around waiting for handouts!

It was time to make something happen.

I called Mama "B," who fed me a bunch of bullshit. She was glad I was home. She missed me to death. Can't wait to see me, etcetera, etcetera. She wished she could help me but she just paid bills and had to buy four new tires for her car.

A bunch of bullshit!

Finally, I said, "Fuck it," and had Sugar Walls give me a ride to East Palo Alto. I'd been on 66th and MacArthur in East Oakland long enough.

She kept asking me why I had an attitude. She may have been very intelligent, but I swore she was dumb as fuck. If asking about my attitude wasn't funny enough, she had the nerve to ask me when I would be back. Instead of laughing at her, I looked right in her eyes and told her, "When I'm not broke."

I stepped out of the car before she could respond. She'd dropped me off at Price's Barber Shop on C Street. I watched her pull off with an attitude, then took in my surroundings.

C Street was popping! At least twelve niggaz were out grinding. The barber shop was "the spot." My uncle Price owned it and my Uncle Pete made sure it ran smooth, with no problems.

The war between The Village, Menlo Park and Midtown ended a little while back, so everybody came to Price's for a cut. The war lasted almost all of the nineties. Now everybody was getting money. I said, "What's up," to a few niggaz I knew then made my way inside. Although I was a Menlo nigga, I had a lot of love from a few cats in the village.

"Mont, what's up, nephew!" Pete stopped cutting the head he was on and stepped to meet me. Wasn't no one-arm gangsta hug, we embraced in a full bear hug.

"What's up, Unc?" He was my mother's youngest brother yet had always been a father to me. Always have, always will be.

"Shit, nephew, you done got big up in there," he told me as he stepped back and looked at me. "When did you get out?"

"Almost a week ago."

"And you're just coming by to say something?" It was more of a scolding than a question.

"Shit, I've been cooped up with Little Mama the whole time, trying to get my mind right." That partially was true.

"Nigga, you was tryna get yo dick right," he joked, and everybody in the shop laughed.

"Your brother just left 'bout ten minutes ago."

"Is that right? How's he doing?" I missed my big brother. I couldn't wait to see his ass.

Pete pulled out his cell phone. "Shit, he doing good, him and your cousins. I'mma call him and tell him you up here."

While he did that, I said hi to Mr. Blackwell, the number-three barber, gave uncle price a hug, then I went outside to smoke a Newport.

Some of the younger cats looked at me, wondering who I was or where I was from, maybe even why I was at the shop. Their attempts at trying to look hard were cute. I was hoping

Clark hurried up before I had to fuck one of them up.

I had money on my mind, not violence. Shit, I had enough of prison to last a lifetime.

Clark pulled into the parking lot in a burnt-orange scraper on twenty-fours, with the system knocking something fierce. He stepped out cleaner than a bitch in a red Monkey outfit, looking like he was happy to see a nigga. "What's up, Mont?" he called out before hugging me like I was his long-lost friend.

"What's up, big brah?" I returned his embrace. Damn, it felt good to see my big brah!

The last time I'd seen him was when I visited him at Elmwood County Jail. That was three years ago. When I visited him, I had just come home from doing five years in the California Youth Authority.

This was the first time we both had been on the streets the same time since I was twelve and he was fourteen.

"Nigga, it's about time you came home. Shit nigga, you been locked up since we was kids. You got to stop fucking with them niggaz you been fucking with and fuck with us, Rogue. It's good right now." From the looks of things, he wasn't lying.

"I hear you, Rogue. We'll see what's good when it's time to rock!" One thing about my brother was he always made it sound good. But the only thing I ever remember my brother ever giving me was a black eye when I was thirteen.

"Rogue, what you doing up here?"

"Waiting on Unc."

"Come with me for a while. Tell Pete you'll be back."

Hell yeah, I could roll with big brah for a while. It had been too long. Plus, I was tired of the same wannabe hard niggaz that were just mean mugging me, jocking brah like he was a rock star.

I dipped in the shop and told Pete I was rolling with Clark.

I made sure to let him know I would be coming back, because I needed to talk with him.

When I went outside, the wannabe hard niggaz were all surrounding brah. When they looked at me, all their looks were different. A couple of them even said, "What's up?" when Clark told them I was his brother. I just ignored them clown ass niggaz.

It wasn't good just a minute ago, so it ain't good now.

We hopped in the whip and got up out of there. For a while, we just rode around listening to music. It was another beautiful, Bay Area summer day. I honestly can't remember what we were listening to, I just remember that it was slapping!

Riding around, I quickly learned my brother was a hood celebrity. We didn't turn on one corner or drive down one street where somebody didn't know him or his car.

It somewhat made me nervous. If everyone knew you and what you drove, you were an easy target. My brother loved the shit though. All our lives, he always wanted to be seen. Wanted people to recognize and notice him. Something told me he was showing off, but I let him enjoy the moment. I was happy for him.

A little while later, we turned down O'Connor Street and pulled up in front of a nice little single-story house. I was cool just sitting back doing me, until he said, "Come on, Rogue."

"Clark, Rogue, I'm not tryna meet nobody. Who lives here?" Before opening his door and climbing out he told me "Rogue, this is my shit, nigga!"

Okay, my nigga was really doing his thang, I thought, as I opened the door and climbed out.

The house was your typical three-bedroom house in the hood. The furniture was of average quality and in average condition. The house was nice and clean which let me know that he was living with a female.

I followed behind him as he walked to one of the back rooms. I could barely make out the faint smell of weed smoke. When we walked in the room, he told me, "Nigga, check this shit out," as he reached into the closet and pulled out a Russian AK-47.

I'm not even going to lie. That bitch looked beautiful. This was the first time I'd ever seen a real-life AK-47. I instantly began thinking of all the mayhem I could cause with that bitch.

Just when my hopes were through the roof, I realized the mothafucka didn't have a clip in it.

"Nigga, where the fuck is the clip at?" I asked, expecting him to pull it right out.

"Got to buy one." The nigga said that shit like he was telling me the time.

"Rogue. What the fuck you buy a gun without a clip for? That was the dumbest shit in the world."

I could sense I'd hurt his feelings by the look on his face. But it was too late for all that shit.

"Nigga, I don't even know why I showed your ass. You ain't got no clue what it's like in the field! What the fuck you buy a gun without a clip for?" he mimicked me. "Nigga, a motherfucker can get a clip easy as fuck! At least I got the 'K,' that's the important part."

I didn't see things the way he did. If niggaz ran up in here right now, that bitch wasn't going to do shit. Yet, if the police were to run up in this bitch, we both were looking at a fed case.

I decided to change the temperature. "Nigga, I ain't gonna lie. Clark, I see you doing your thang. Riding around this mothafucka like the president." I stroked his ego a little bit.

"One day, Rogue, I'm gonna be the president of East Palo Alto," he vowed.

"Shit, nigga, what about Boi?" Boi was one of our cousins who was hell-bent on doing the same thing. He and Clark were closer to brothers than Clark and I could ever be.

"Shit, Rogue, everybody gets a run. I'll let Boi have his run, but when it's my turn, it's my turn. Straight up!"

I could hear a conviction in his voice I had never heard before.

We kicked it in front of his house for a while, chopping it up, talking about back in the day, when a couple of Clark's homeboys came by. We took turns smoking a couple of blunts, while we chopped it up some more.

When it was time to head back to the barber shop, we rode in his whip listening to some niggaz called Big Timers, rap about gator boots and Gucci suits. They couldn't pay their rent, but they were still fly. With all the flossing he was doing, I figured my brotha would be quick to set a nigga out. What better way to say, "I'm up," than to put one of your niggaz on?

So, I asked him to put a nigga "on," so I could do me. To my surprise, he told me it was good!

I swear to God, this mothafucka went inside his pocket and pulled out fifty dollars, fifty-faggot-ass dollars. I was so pissed off, I didn't know who to feel sorry for, him or me.

The words to Jay-Z's song, "Cry," came to mind.

I'm a man with pride, you don't do shit like that. Before getting out of the car, I told him if all he could throw a nigga was fifty dollars, then he was just as bad as me and needed the money more. He had the nerve to think I was tripping.

"What's up, nephew? You niggaz get caught up?" Uncle Pete asked me as he came out of the shop with a Black & Mild in one hand and a lighter in the other.

"I guess you can say that." I caught Pete up on everything we had just gotten into.

As we talked, he lit and smoked his Black and I fired up a

Newport. When I told Pete about the fifty dollars, he was so shocked all he could say was, "He did what! Naaw, nephew, that nigga ain't that scandalous." Pete just shook his head for a minute then added, "All that money him and your cousins got, and all that nigga gave you was fifty motherfucking dollars."

"Shit, I didn't take that shit. Unc, that was flat out disrespectful. What the fuck am I supposed to do with fifty dollars? Especially from a nigga that just spent the past few hours flossing like he was Deion mothafuck'n Sanders."

Pete started laughing so hard, he began choking. We chopped it up for about thirty more minutes before he got serious and asked me, "So, nephew, what are you going to do?"

"Honestly, Unc, I don't know. A nigga ain't trying to go back to prison, but I'll be damned if I'm out here living like a bum." Since Pete was more like a father figure to me than an uncle, I always kept it real with him.

"Then what you need, nephew?" He didn't hesitate to ask me.

"If I jump back in with both feet planted, Unc, all I need is a quarter to get off my feet." Shit, honesty was the best policy.

By then, Uncle Price came out of the back and locked the shop up. The sun had gone down almost thirty-something minutes ago. Pete and I both said our goodbyes to Uncle Price. After Price left, we climbed inside Pete's gold Taurus and finished talking.

"Nephew, you know I haven't sold dope since the nineties, when I went to prison. I'm not built for all that penitentiary shit, being around a bunch of niggaz. I need to be around some bitches. But I'm not about to let one of my sister's kids be out here white around the mouth like Al Jolson and his pockets touching." He pulled out his cell phone again and dialed a number.

"Come on, nephew, I got you," he said after hanging up the phone.

We headed to the Light Trees, an apartment complex that everyone referred to as the projects or simply "the jets." Pete had called my cousin B.A, who had just come home himself from prison, but was doing his thang.

When we got there, B.A. and my little cousin Freeman were playing John Madden on PlayStation. Before I'd left, my little cousin was just Freeman Owens III, now he went by the name, Tut-Tut.

B.A. and I did some catching up, but it wasn't a social visit, so we got down to business. Unc paid cuzzo (cousin) for a quarter ounce of crack for me. I got more than I had expected, because B.A. threw me an extra quarter since I had just come home.

To me, that was some real gangsta shit. But B.A. had always been that way with me. Even though I never really asked anybody for anything, whenever he knew I needed something, he was there for a nigga.

Before Pete and I left, Tut came up to me with a serious look on his face and told me, "Voorheeze, on some real shit, dad if you ever need a nigga that's 'BTA,' all you got to do is call me and it's good."

"Nigga, what the fuck is BTA?" I'd never heard the term.

He made a hand gesture like he was squeezing the trigger when he replied, "Bout that action, dad."

This little mothafucka couldn't have been no more than fifteen or sixteen, but the look in his young eyes dared me not to take him seriously.

Back in the car, Unc told me he had a closet full of new clothes for me if I could get my little female to bring me by his spot to pick them up. I let him know for sure, I would be there to pick them up.

As we rode, Unc was bumping some nigga named Tyrese. That was one thing about Pete, he was as gangsta as they came when he needed to be. Other than those times that called for some gangsta shit, he was as smooth as they came, a real ladies' man.

I ended up having him drop me off in the Safeway parking lot in San Jose. Now that I had some work, it was time to go work. I swear to God, I love my uncle to death!

Just before I stepped out of the whip, he asked me what I was about to do. I kept it one hundred and told him I needed a couple of razor blades and a box of sandwich bags. I was about to run up there and get my five-finger discount on. Pete reached inside his pocket, broke me off another five hundred dollars and told me to be easy.

The night was as black as tar and as cold as ice, which made them identical twins to my heart. A Siamese threesome. Yeah, I was on my hustle shit!

I bought a box of razor blades and a box of sandwich bags. Now, I'm not going to even sit here and lie, I stole that shit. But I did buy me a pack of Newports, some of that deli chicken, extra crispy and a bottle of Brisk iced tea.

I left Safeway and walked two miles down El Camino, until I reached the Alameda Motel, my old stomping grounds. It was a little after nine thirty when I checked in. The Alameda Motel was your typical, roach-infested, dope fiend living grounds. The rooms were cheap and so was the furniture. I wouldn't be caught dead sleeping in the bed, that was no doubt full of bed bugs, dried semen, and God only knows what else.

I got a room for forty-five dollars. It was Room 8 in the back-left side of the motel. When you drove in, it was one of them joints that was built in a straight line like an alleyway with rooms on both sides. I was happy to get Room 8, because

I could see the entire property out the window, who came in and who went out.

My chicken was still a little warm when I finally walked into the room. I turned on the TV and knocked down the fried chicken and potato wedges, with some of them single packets of ranch salad dressing. Then washed them down with the tea.

After eating, I jumped straight into the lab. Downtown San Jose was the hottest place in California to sell dope and because of that, the crack rocks were the size of nothing. I mean literally, a twenty-dollar-rock was the size of a kernel of corn. I swear to God, I chopped sixty-two rocks off each quarter.

It took me over an hour to cut up and individually wrap all one hundred and twenty-four rocks. When I was done though, I had me a nice bundle, twenty-four hundred and eighty dollars' worth. I stayed up all night going over my next move.

**** N. D. ****

CHAPTER 13

The next morning, I was up bright and early ready to hit the block. Considering I sat in the hard, wooden chair fully dressed all night, I didn't sleep much. I just dozed off and on until around 8:00 a.m.

We sold dope all throughout Downtown San Jose from 1st Street all the way down to 15th Street and from Santa Clara Street all the way down to St. James Park. The main spot was between 1st and 2nd Streets, along Santa Clara Street.

I just walked around observing, seeing who was who and what was what, for a while. I was rolling a blunt in one of the alleyways when O.G. Red called out my name. Red was a dope fiend that used to bring me money before I caught my prison beef. He was a cool dude with a lot of game and finesse about himself.

"Man, I knew that was you when I saw you walking down San Fernando Street. But I remember how you liked to do your recon before you hit the block, so I left you be. Here you are live in the flesh, my mothafuck'n partna, Smooth!" Anyone could hear the excitement in his voice.

He had reason to be excited too. We made a lot of money together three years ago, and Red smoked a lot of crack for free off of our little set-up. With a gleam shining in his eyes Red asked me, "So tell me, Smooth, are you gonna let old Red play running back like we used to?"

Everyone knew my name was Voorheeze, but back in the day, the ladies used to always call me Smooth. They said it was because I was always on some Al B. Sure!, New Edition type shit. Before long, everyone downtown began calling me Smooth.

"Red, you know me, the game's always the same. The only things that change is the suckas and the lames. I'm ready to get the money, Big Homie, if you're ready," I told him as I handed him the lit blunt I was smoking.

Our old system was simple. I always gave Red his first rock for free. Afterwards, every thirty dollars he brought my way, I would give him either a ten-dollar-rock or ten dollars in cash. The system worked beautifully for both of us. I swear to God, Red would bring me two sales every ten minutes. Do the math. You have six, ten-minute intervals in one hour. That's sixty of them in ten hours, at thirty each wop. So, on any given Sunday, Red would bring me an average of eighteen thousand a day. This was separate from the clientele I sold to.

After the blunt was gone, I set up shop. It was slow going for a minute. After all, I'd been gone for three years. To a lot of the dope fiends, I was a new face. But once word got out that I had the biggest rocks in the area, everything picked up.

It felt good to be back in the hustle and bustle of things. In under an hour, I already had over six hundred dollars in my pocket. A nigga was feeling good. When I got the cream from B.A. last night, he also threw me an eighth of Grapes with it. That's how I got the blunt I was smoking with Red.

Coming out of the liquor store on Santa Clara Street, a fiend walked up to me, wanting to spend eighty dollars I had to get that. We stepped to the bus stop off to the right and I served him.

I left the bus stop and went right back in the liquor store. I added one of my own twenty-dollar-bills to the four the white boy (dope fiend) gave me and traded all five for a hundred-dollar-bill.

The owner of the liquor store knew what I was doing. He didn't trip because every time I got a twenty-dollar-bill from someone I remotely felt suspicious about, I came to his store and bought something like a soda, box of Newports, box of Phillies or something. I did this in case one of the bills someone gave me was marked. I wouldn't have the bill on me.

With the new hundred-dollar-bill in my pocket, I left the store for what had to be the twelfth or thirteenth time that morning. I looked up at the glaring sun and smiled, happy not to be in Crescent City, California.

I was getting ready to turn the corner onto 2nd Street when all of my instinct and intuition started ringing like a high school bell. Instead of stopping and analyzing the feeling, I walked head high and turned the corner.

The sight before my eyes almost made me shit my pants. There were five or six police cars and two paddy wagons parked at different angles, blocking off Second Street. Something like fifteen, sixteen cops had a bunch of the young hustlahs lined up against the wall being frisked and searched at gunpoint.

I knew to panic would be the wrong thing to do. So, without breaking my stride, I reached into my pants pocket and pulled out my cigarettes. Like any other nosy bystanders, I made sure to pay just enough, to draw any attention to myself as I observed the scene.

My strategy must've worked because, although a couple of cops looked at me curiously, no one bothered me nor tried to stop me as I walked to one of the benches and stood by to wait for the next Light Rail train to come.

A couple of the hustlahs gave me the evil eye, mad because I hadn't gotten wrapped up in the sweep. Those were the bitch niggaz.

The look in the rest of the hustlahs eyes was the look you find in real niggaz' eyes. They were just happy one of us got away.

I smoked my cigarette, thinking about my next move. I literally had a sack with about twenty or so rocks still on me, inside my pockets. If one of the cops did decide to fuck with me, I was sure to have problems. I'm talking, back to the penitentiary problems.

Some white chick walked by me with an ass so phat I had to look at that thang. Now, I personally don't fuck with pink meat, but all the ladies know I'm an ass man! I would admire any woman with a nice big ass. Hey! That's just me. Doesn't mean I'm fucking, but I am for sure looking.

I didn't notice the white, redneck, racist looking cop watching me admiring all that ass. I noticed him the moment he began walking towards my direction. The look on the cop's face told me I fucked up by looking at the white chick!

My heart instantly started racing. I could feel the pores on my forehead open up as my body temperature elevated. My very first thought was to get rabbit and dodge him on foot. He was about ten feet away from me. It was decision time. Now or never! Take him on a chase or play the cards where they lay.

"Hey, brother! I'm sorry we're late, but Mom wouldn't let us out of the house until we had something to eat." I looked to my right to see who was speaking and got the shock of a lifetime.

It was my god-sister Edwina. Her and Quesha, one of her home girl's, were both pushing strollers with babies in them walking up to me.

I hadn't seen Edwina since like four months before I caught my prison term. Back then, Quesha and I used to fuck around a little, but nothing serious. I was happy as dog shit to see the two of them. Instantly, my swag kicked into gear. Without missing a beat, I smiled and gave her a hug.

"What's up, little sis? I was mad at you for having me wait up here for so long. But now, thinking how Mom is, I should've known it was her fault that you were late." Yeah, I was full-on Damon Wayans' acting mode.

After hugging Edwina, I further played it off by leaning down, kissing the little baby and playing with it. Out of my peripheral vision, I watched the cop hesitate, then stop as he assessed the situation. I knew his mind was trying to analyze and dissect the scene before his eyes.

To put the icing on the cake, so to speak, I walked over to Q and gave her a hug and a kiss on the cheek. The warmth in which we all greeted each other was genuine enough to alter whatever plan ole boy had in his mind.

The Light Rail train came a minute later. Giving the cop no time to rethink his decision, the five of us hopped on the train quicker than Flash.

"Damn, bro, your ass has been gone forever. I see all that prison food done blew you the fuck up too!" Edwina said as soon as we all found our seats.

"God damn, Dwina, I ain't been happier to see somebody than I am at seeing you right now." Shit, I was so happy, I could kiss her.

"Yeah, my nigga. Cause that white boy was for sure going to fuck with you, my nigga, behind the way you were looking at that white bitch with that big ole ass." Q said this and we all started laughing.

When the laughing died down, Edwina asked me, "How long you been out, Voorheeze? Cause I know you about to get it popping."

We got off Light Rail a block away. In response to her question, I suggested we go to Johnny Rockets and grab a bite to eat. We could talk business over there.

Johnny Rockets was one of them old school burger joints like on the movie, *Pulp Fiction*. The one where John Travolta got the five-dollar shake. It was right around the corner. Its food and milk shakes were just as good as John Travolta described in the movie.

Along the way, I found out both of the little girls were Q's, that she had by some nigga she started fucking with after I left.

I couldn't help but to notice how thick she had gotten. Edwina caught me looking at Q and laughed. "Boy, you need to quit!"

"It ain't even that kind of party, sis." And it really wasn't. Even in prison, niggaz keep their ears to the street. I had already heard all about Q and her baby daddy.

I bought all of us food, even the kids. As we ate, I laid everything out for them. I was on a mission to blow up like dynamite and was taking everybody close to me, with me.

They liked my plan and was on board. We decided to meet back on the block at 5:30 p.m. It was too hot to bust moves now and if I was really trying to do something big, I was going to need more work. Like Ice Cube, Mack-10 and Dub-C, we were three the hard way!

I left them at Johnny Rockets and caught the Light Rail to Mama "B's" (my mom's) house.

My mom and I kicked it for a couple of hours. It was good seeing her for real, for real. Mama "B" had lived a hard life. When I say she's been through and done it all, I mean that shit literally. My mother was the definition of a real "gangstress." She'd been robbed, kidnapped, shot at, stabbed and raped. She would knock out women and men. She has been to county jail, state and federal prison. She'd been a true queen pin, only to fall and become a dope fiend.

No matter what she'd been, she was always my queen and my everything. Even when she messed up.

Mama was mad that I hadn't come directly to see her, but she got over it. Before I left, she let me have her voicemail pager. A must-have for true D-Boi's!

I gave Mama "B" a kiss on the lips and a bear hug before I left. It was time to make it happen.

**** N. D. ****

De'Kari

CHAPTER 14

After seeing Mama "B," I jumped on the 22 El Camino Real. The 22 ran from San Jose to Palo Alto, stopping on almost every other corner along the way. It takes almost two hours to get there, but what could I do? I didn't have a car. So, I stayed on the bus.

An hour and some change later, we pulled into the Palo Alto train station. I was tired of sitting down and even more tired of sightseeing through the window.

The problem with catching the 22 to Palo Alto was, no one would come and pick me up from the station. It was sort of an unwritten law that niggaz from East Palo Alto didn't go to Palo Alto. Period!

I wasn't tripping. I walked the three or four miles it took to get to East Palo Alto from Palo Alto, with a pocket full of money, a shoe full of dope and a plan.

Once I finally made it to the hood without getting pulled over or harassed, I found a pay phone and called B.A. Fifteen minutes later, I was climbing into the passenger seat of a red Chevy Camaro.

"Damn, Mont. You're finished with all of that shit already?" he asked me as he pulled out of the Chevron gas station on University.

"Shit. I ain't gone front, big cousin, I still got about half of one left. But the block on fire right now and since a nigga can't make no money right now, I figured I would get right so when it's time to get money, I can get it right. You feel me!" I said with pride.

I've never been the type of dude that tried to impress niggaz. Yet, for some reason, I always wanted to impress B.A.

"Look at Mont! Tryna be on some Harry-O, Freeway Rick shit!" He shouted and then laughed. "Alright then, little nigga, how much are you tryna get?"

"How much are you going to charge me for the whole onion?" An onion is an ounce.

This got his attention. "Okay. Okay. I see you ain't playing, cousin. You know right, now they going for five-fifty, but since you're serious about your grind and you just came home, I'll give it to you for five hundred, the next five times you come and get one."

I thought about his deal for a moment and I thought about how much money I had. I remember years ago my cousin Boi once told me a true hustler would spend every dollar, because the work always made you more money. I had fifteen hundred in my pocket, another rack stashed in my room and still about a five-hundred-dollar count on me.

With Boi's words in my head, I made a counteroffer. "You say five hundred, will you give me three for twelve hundred right now?"

"Come on, Mont! Nigga, we family! I got you, Rogue. You got twelve on you right now?" When I nodded my head, all he said was I had to ride with him to the Light Trees.

The walk back to the train station was nerve-racking. With over three ounces of crack cocaine on me, I walked each block praying to God. Asking God over and over, to please not allow me to get stopped by the police.

Normally, the police fucked with anything black they caught anywhere in Palo Alto, which was why we stayed the fuck away from Palo Alto. As far away as we could.

God was with me though. I made it back to the motel incident-free. It was still early, so I immediately got down to business, chopping up my white gold. I only chopped up two ounces, because I didn't want to miss that 6 p.m. rush. From 6 to 7 p.m. was one of the rushes, because everyone getting off work and needed to stop and get their nightly fix.

By the time I made it back to "the block" (First Street and Santa Clara Street), Edwina and Q were already there, minus the strollers and babies. They were having a good time with my white boy partner, Dollar and a few other niggaz.

Before I went in, Dollar and I had been real tight. He turned his head in my direction as I approached.

"Oh shit! They done fucked around and let a real nigga out, just in time for a real nigga holiday!" he called out all excitedly.

Dollar was a smooth ass mothafucka. Back in the day, the mothafucka thought he was the singer Jon B. He had the look, the pretty boy Jon B. beard with a thin ass chin strap and a slicker mouthpiece than Sugar Wolf Pimp. No lie, E-40 Fonzarelli ain't had shit on Dollar.

"Nigga, I had to see what's up with my brother from another mother. On top of that, you know I stay billy goat hungry and I hear this is where the paper at." As if to confirm my theory, a dope fiend walked up trying to spend forty dollars. Dollar jumped on the sale. That gave me the time to pull Edwina to the side and tell her I needed her to walk with me, to find somewhere to stash some of my shit.

Edwina and I talked as we walked through the alleyways. It gave me a chance to run down to her how we were about to get down. It was a little difficult, because every nigga we passed broke their necks to get a look at Edwina!

I'm not even going to lie, my little sis was superbad, with a body to match. And every time a nigga looked our way, I looked his. But I was just on some "safety and security" shit. Edwina and I had never crossed that line. She really was little sis. But the niggaz passing us by didn't know that. So, I was on point.

My strategy was simple. I'd cut my rocks a little bit bigger this time. Instead of chopping sixty off a quarter, I cut forty-eight, which would still bring me nine-sixty. Edwina and Q were going to be the ones that sold it. They each would have their own bundle and would get twenty-five off of every hundred.

All I would do is be on point with security and manage the money. Out of the three ounces, I'd chopped up one. That, with what I had left over from this morning, I had a little over two hundred, twenty-dollar-rocks. Nigga, I was ready to get it poppin! By the time T'Rida came home, I was going to be in a nice little place. As sure as a bear shitting in the woods and wiping his ass with a rabbit. Nigga, I was going to be on it like shit!

It was a nice plan and we executed it well.

The block was jumping so hard, a nigga almost couldn't keep up with the money. That was, almost!

More men went to Edwina because of her looks. And they ended up spending more. But Q was a go-getter. She had hustle about her. Plus, Edwina spent time flirting with her customers to get them to spend more. Which meant Q was out-selling Edwina two to one.

The fiends were coming so much that a nigga had to dip back to the Alameda to get some more work.

I had about another two-thousand-dollar count chopped and bagged by the time Edwina paged me on the voicemail pager I got from Mama "B." That was my cue to let me know they only had ten rocks left.

With my fingers numb from all the crack I'd been touching, and body tingling from all the money I was making, I hurried to the bus stop and jumped on the first 22 back to the block. A nigga named Jason Voorheeze was chasing the American Dream in a real way.

When I got back to Edwina and Q, that two-hundred-dollar count was down to sixty dollars. I'm not going to lie. They were doing their Dougie! I asked them if they wanted to go and get a bite to eat. Simultaneously, they both told me I was out my crazy ass mind. They were getting that paper and wasn't letting up.

I'd gotten a message on my voicemail, so I used a pay phone, not too far away from where we were to check the message. Surprisingly, it was a message from Stacy.

According to the message, a friend of hers had flown in from Florida. Ordinarily, I wouldn't have given a fuck. However, according to the message, her friend was a stripper and she wanted her to dance for me.

Now, I don't know just what the average dude would've thought or how he would've taken the message. But all I heard was her stripper friend was in town and they were trying to do the most. I had never had a threesome before, but I was sure about to!

I called the number she'd called me from, only to find out it was to the lobby of the DoubleTree Hotel. The clerk behind the desk wouldn't give me her room number, no matter what I did. So, I hung up and hoped she would leave another message.

My niggaz B-Real, Dollar, Lucky Lucciano, Tone, and J.W. were all out that night with a slew of honeys. Some bad, a couple superbad and a few ratchet, but all having fun.

The nightlife in downtown San Jose was bonkers. Money came hand over fist. There were a few clubs downtown. Clubgoers needed their party treats too. For us, the block was our club and we partied hard. During the day, you would see a hundred cops downtown, but at night it was almost an open free for all... Almost!

"Yieeeekitee!" When I heard that sound, it brought me back to my prison time. The sound was Q letting me know she sold the last rock. That signaled the block we were out of dope and time to close shop.

When I collected the money, I had too much money on me to be on the streets with no banger. Voorheeze wasn't no dummy! Instead of kicking it, I had them walk with me to the Voodoo Lounge. It was one of the clubs downtown. The cool thing about the Voodoo Lounge was it had a patio in the back of the club. This was our destination.

We walked inside the club arm in arm, all three of us. I did this because the Voodoo Lounge was really a gay bar. I didn't want anybody to get it fucked up. I had two bad bitches on my arm and a look on my face that wasn't approachable.

When we found a nice little table out back, a waitress took our drink order.

When she left, Q looked at me and said, "Nigga, yo ass gone stop acting like you don't know a bitch, Voorheeze."

I was in the middle of counting their money out when she said that shit. I was thrown completely off.

"Q, what in the hell are you talking about? I'm tryna get y'all bread right now."

"Nigga, I ain't tripping off my chips. I know you gone come correct. All day, you've been avoiding a bitch like I got bubonic plague or shit, my nigga! Damn! I mean, like for real, you don't think a bitch missed you? Come on, my nigga, damn!" She let her emotions go.

I don't know where that shit was coming from, but it was right there in a nigga'z face.

"Aww, hell naaw, that's my clue to excuse myself." Edwina scooted her chair back, then reached over and grabbed two twenties out of my hand. "Minus this from my take. I'm going to find me a nice little tender to take home while you two talk out whatever y'all got to talk about. I love you, brother. Thank you for putting some money in a bitch's purse." With that, Edwina stood up and disappeared among a sea of bodies.

"Lil Mama, you can't be serious?" I was stunned.

"My nigga, what you mean? Like for real, my nigga. Do a bitch got to spell it out for you?" She was beginning to look pissed off.

I was glad the waitress chose right then to bring us our drinks. It gave me time to reconfigure some shit. I took a long swallow of my Don Julio Añejo and looked at her.

She was beautiful. Yet, she had two babies by Ty'Reke bitch ass and was still low-key fucking with him. Which meant she was poisonous fruit.

"Come on, Lil Mama. You got a whole ass baby daddy, whom you're still fucking with, I might add. Yeah, it's good seeing you, and from looking at your body, your two girls did you some good. Still, I ain't never been a man to mess with another man's shit." It was that simple.

I wouldn't want a nigga to mess with my woman. So, I didn't mess with another man's woman.

Q and I talked for another fifteen minutes or so, before Edwina came back. She couldn't do nothing but respect my position, like I respected hers. I didn't have the heart to tell her that the word on the streets was her nigga was snitching. It wasn't my place. I guess she'll find out when she reads this book.

I gave both of them eleven hundred dollars. We all had another round of drinks and then left. I walked them to their bus stop and waited with them until their bus came. The I jumped on the last 22 El Camino Real and headed to the motel.

**** **N. D.** ****

De'Kari

CHAPTER 15

One of the bus stops for the 22 was almost directly across the street from the motel. No sooner had I stepped off the bus, my pager went off. It pissed me off because I'd recognized the number as being the number that Stacy called me from earlier. Thoughts of all the freaky shit I could do to the two of them played in my head.

The problem with all that was a phone. The phones in the raggedy motel usually didn't work. The closest phone that worked was damn near a mile and a half down the street, back the way I'd just come from. Had I gotten the page five minutes earlier, I could've gotten off the bus in time to be close to the phones.

It was a nice warm night out, but I was too tired to enjoy it. Since I'm a young perverted nigga, I wasn't too tired to walk my ass back down the street though!

I checked my voicemail, ready for some action. Disappointment set in once I'd listened to my message. Yeah, it was from ole girl and yeah, she was saying it was good to come through. However, she didn't tell me where she was, nor did she leave me a number where I could call her. Instead, I called her voicemail pager.

"Aye, what's up? I got your message and it's all good on my end, but I don't have a cell phone. So, page me back and leave me a message with a phone number, so I can call you and we hook up." I hung the phone up and lit a cigarette, waiting for her to respond.

I stood at the pay phone for at least fifteen minutes. Waiting for my pager to go off. Eventually I got tired of waiting and walked back to the motel.

I swear to God, I'd just opened the door to my room when my pager went off. I grabbed the pager out of my pocket and checked the number. Frustration caused me to chuckle when I noticed the number.

It was the same number again. I'd like to say that I said, "Fuck her," and ignored the page. Truth is I was young, optimistic, and horny!

Before I did anything, I walked over to the bed and retrieved the bag underneath the pillow. It was where I kept the rest of the work. After grabbing a little work, I was out the door back to the pay phone. I grabbed some work because the fiends didn't sleep, so I had to be ready at all times.

I took my ass all the way back down to the Kwik Stop where the pay phones were, only to get the same results as earlier, while waiting for the page that never came. I did sell sixty dollars to some white dude another thirty-five dollars to a prostitute.

Mama "B" was still on my mind, at least the things she had to do in order to get her next hit. Because of this, I ended up giving the prostitute sixty dollars' worth of work for her thirty-five dollars.

I only waited ten minutes before leaving this time. I wasn't too mad, because I at least made some money. The majority of my money, which was thirty-eight hundred dollars, was beneath the inside soles of my shoe. I still had about four or five hundred and some change in my pockets.

An average person would've learned their lesson by now. Unfortunately, I'm not the average person, nor do I learn lessons when it comes to freaky shit. So, when the pager went off a third time as I started to chop up the rest of the dope, I walked my stupid, gullible ass to the pay phone for the third time.

Twenty minutes after leaving her a rather fucked-up voicemail, I was walking down the streets. Smoking a Newport angrily calling her every degrading, disrespectful name I could think of. I don't know why, but right then Lisa popped in my mind. I found myself thinking that if I was with Lisa, I wouldn't be out on the streets at that time of night chasing some phantom pussy.

The streets were damn near empty by now. The occasional vehicle would drive by every now and then, but for the most part, it was just me on the street.

"Say, my man. You got it?" Some cat rolled up on me on a ten-speed bike and asked.

"What you looking for?" I responded.

"Man, I got a twenty. I need a dub of some cream," he called out.

I served him and kept on about my business, walking back to the room and thinking about what life would be like with Lisa.

As I was approaching the corner, a gray Dodge Caravan was reaching the same corner. It was one of them soccer mom minivans. I stopped on the curb and made a gesture with my hands, letting the driver know I was giving them the right of way.

In an instant, faster than a New York minute, the van swerved and came to a stop right in front of me. The back door slid open and my eyes widened. I was staring down the barrels of two very big ass guns. The niggaz holding the guns were trying to look all hard and shit, like I fucked their mother, but I could see the bitch in their eyes right away.

"Break yo'self, nigga!" the light-skinned nigga said, trying his hardest to sound tough.

"My nigga, you got me fucked up! Nigga, I'm Jason mothafuck'n Voorheeze and I'd be damn if one of you bitch ass San Jose niggaz gone rob me. You better off finding the next nigga." I stared his punk ass right in his bitch-ass eyes.

He looked over to the dark nigga. That nigga looked like he was more interested in sucking my dick, than robbing me. Picture that!

Me, Jason Voorheeze getting robbed by a van full of homosexuals.

That shit had me pissed off. I mean, come on. For real! I'mma an ex-con, a felon nigga, but I'm supposed to empty my pockets for Wanda and Sha-nay-nay?

When the dark nigga looked up towards the passenger, whom I couldn't see because of the tinted windows, my nuts really dropped, and my courage grew.

"What the fuck you looking up there for, pussy! You're the one with the mothafuck'n gun. Bust a mothafuck'n move, you ole bitch ass, San Jose ass nigga!" I challenged.

In response, the front passenger window rolled down. The eyes that stared at me would make the Devil himself shit his pants. They were filled with anger, hatred, death and despair.

"You talking real mothafuck'n slick right about now. You ole bitch-ass nigga!" She upped an all-black, baby Bin Laden M-1 and cocked that bitch. "Since you got a problem with San Jose niggaz, strip, nigga! Or watch this San Jose bitch turn you into a ballerina."

A mothafucka can say what they want to say. But looking into her eyes, all I saw was death. The death of the lives she's already taken, as well as my death if I didn't get naked. I came up out that shit like it was on fire.

I still mumbled and talked shit up under my breath. As I did, I handed her my clothes piece by piece. Out the corner of my eye, I saw the dark nigga looking at me like I was a giant Snickers bar. My blood boiled.

"That's right! Keep on talking shit, but make sure you take all that shit off. Them little cute boxers you got on too," she tormented me.

I stood there on the corner, asshole butt-naked, mean mugging the little bitch. I was pissed off and confused. Pissed that I had got caught slipping and confused because a bitch with that much gangsta needed to be on my team.

"I know you're not testing my 'G,' nigga! Kick me them sneakers too. This bitch ass, San Jose bitch need them."

For a split second, I thought about running. I had too much money in my shoes. I didn't care about the few hundred in my pocket. But it was almost four G's in my shoes.

My common sense reminded me of the carnage I'd seen in her eyes.

Reluctantly, in the end, I was the bitch. I came out of the shoes and handed them to her.

"Nigga, what the fuck are these?" She held the shoes up and inspected them. Her face was screwed up like my feet stank. "Newport! Nigga, what kind of nigga wears some shoes called Newport?" They all started laughing like we were watching *Def Comedy Jam* or something.

I wasn't laughing though. I was ready to knock this little pretty ass, high yellow bitch, smooth the fuck out.

"Bitch ass nigga! You had to buy these at Payless. Ain't no Foot Locker selling no fucking Newport shoes. If you don't take these cheap ass, bitch nigga shoes!"

Before I could blink, she threw the shoes back at me. One hit me in the chest, while the other cracked me in the side of my head. I could hear them all laughing long after the van pulled out.

This time I was laughing too.

Thank God that pretty little demon bitch didn't take my shoes. The cool night air blowing against my balls reminded me of my current predicament. I picked up both shoes and made my way back to my room barefoot.

I was thinking God must have really been on my side, since I made it all the way back to the motel without running into anyone. Not even a single car drove by me.

My thoughts quickly changed as I approached my room. As I walked down the street, I tried to figure out just how I was going to get in the room.

It appeared that someone had solved that problem for me. The door to my room was slightly ajar. I rushed into the room with no worry or concern about my safety. I was only concerned with all the dope that was left in the room.

I don't know why I had any hopes of my shit being there, because it wasn't!

Fuck!

I'd made forty-five hundred off of the ounce I chopped up earlier. That, plus the eleven hundred I'd given the girls. I made sixty-six hundred off of one ounce. Whoever broke into my room made off with more than an ounce and a half. I could've made seven thousand easily off of that.

Fuck!

I was so mad that I could kill somebody! First, I got humiliated and stripped by a female. Now this shit! The damage I would do now if I had a hand cannon.

I paced the room back and forth like an angry lion. Butt-ass naked with the lights off and the door wide open. I was so angry, the faces of Dawoo, Damu, Kool Aide and bunch of other mothafuckas I had killed flashed before my eyes.

Shit just got real!

CHAPTER 16

After a while, a little of my sanity began to return. With that sanity, so did my ability to make rational decisions. The first of which was to grab one of the sheets and wrap it around my waist. I still needed to pace as I tried to calm down. The cool night air played a part in soothing the beast that was raging inside of me.

Movement outside caught my attention. I boldly approached the door to see who just walked by. If I was lucky, it would be whoever robbed me. I was ready to get off in someone's ass!

When I got to the open doorway, the only person that I saw was the prostitute I'd given the blessing to a little earlier. She looked to be in a world of her own, high as a satellite.

"Hey auntie?" I called out to her.

I don't know if she recognized me or not, but when she saw the sheet wrapped around me and my exposed chest, she turned completely around and bee-lined in my direction.

"What's up, daddy?" she asked me when she got near.

"Let me rap with you for a minute. I got a proposition for you that'll put some money in your pockets." I stepped aside, allowing her room to walk inside.

As soon as I closed the door, she asked me, "So what's on your mind, sweetheart?"

When I turned around, she was looking me up and down, licking her lips. Although we stood this close earlier when I sold her the dope, my mind was elsewhere then. In the light of the room, seeing her fully for the first time, I could tell that in another life she used to be beautiful. The years of drug use, prostituting, and survival of the street life, left her a mere shell of the beautiful woman she used to be.

"I'm flattered, auntie, but it ain't even that kind of party. I'm not—" Before I could finish, she cut me off.

"Baby, it's okay if you're shy or a little bit scared of all of this." She pivoted and stuck her hip out. At the same time, she slapped her huge ass. "But, believe me sugar, you're going to love every minute of it. You better believe Miss Paradise will definitely give you something to remember."

I was beginning to lose my patience, even with all that ass she had. I took a deep breath to calm my emotions. When I spoke, I was as calm as a pond in the spring.

"Look, Paradise, I know you're feeling good off of what I sold you a minute ago. But please, auntie, I need some clothes. If you can find me some clothes, I'll pay you more than if you let me bend you over that desk and have it my way with you." I didn't have time for no bullshit. If the sun came up and I didn't have any clothes, I was going to be in deep shit.

She licked her lips again and thought about what I'd just said. I could see the wheels in her mind spinning. While she thought, she rocked back and forth on her feet.

"So, all you want is some clothes?"

"That's all I want, auntie."

"You don't want no pussy?" She kind of looked disappointed.

"Naaw, auntie, I'm good. If I'm stuck in this room asshole butt-naked when the sun comes up, I'm going to be up shit creek without a paddle." I decided to make her feel better. I looked her up and down and licked my lips. "It's not that a nigga wouldn't mind getting a taste of all that chocolate you got. But I got to stay focused on the business at hand."

"And if mama gets you some clothes, you gonna take care of me?"

"Exactly, lil mama."

"Okay, I'll take care of you. But at least let Miss Paradise get a small bump to make her right." I'll be damned if she didn't reach into her bra and pull out a burnt stem, a used crack pipe.

"Lil mama, I got cash, but I ain't got…" Just then, I remembered the sack I had for Red.

Earlier, when I came back to the room to cut the two-thousand-dollar count, I didn't want to get Red's sack mixed up with the count, so I put it up.

I turned around and walked to the closet. I was hoping they didn't take the time to fuck with the closet!

My mind was so focused on seeing if the dope was there, I forgot all about the sheet. I opened the closet, which looked empty. Then I stood on my tiptoes and reached my hand all the way to the way to the back of the shelf up top. The sheet fell off my body.

When my hand touched the bundle, a smile spread across my face. Even though a nigga got jacked, somehow it felt like I was the one who got over, since they didn't find this. It might sound crazy, but when a nigga takes a loss, a win is a win.

"Lord Jesus, help me," she called out when I turned around.

I opened the sack and grabbed three rocks and gave them to her. That took her mind off my body. Paradise wasted no time forcing one of the rocks into her stem. I didn't trip, I let her blast off and do her. She smoked the entire rock, while doing a shimmy like she was coming on herself.

After taking the last hit, she assured me she was going to hook me up.

**** N. D.****

While you're in the joint, you hear almost every lie known to man, and even some that aren't. Almost everybody and their mama was balling out of control. Yet them be the same niggaz that will turn around and ask to bum a twenty-cent soup or a fifty-cent bar of soap. Nigga, you was pushing Beamers, Benzes, and Vett's, but you can't afford fifty cent to wash your ass? Fuck outta here!

Another one of my favorites, was niggaz talking how much pussy they were getting. From the baddest women in the city too. Wasn't nobody in the joint fucking on hoodrats or boppers. And you better not mention jacking off on the streets to a nigga that was locked up. He'd take that as a sign of disrespect. He was getting way too much pussy on the street to be having to beat his dick.

Fuck that! Not me, though!

A nigga could say what they want to about Jason Voorheeze, I don't give a fuck! I was in the shower fantasizing about Janet Jacme and Belladona going ham on my dick. While I was dreaming the perfect fantasy in my head, I was beating my dick.

Real nigga shit!

I'd seen too much ass today, so I was doing my thang. A knock came from the door, fucking up my concentration, just as Bridget the midget entered the fantasy and bent over in front of me. My nigga, I always wanted to fuck a big butt midget.

I snatched one of them little janky ass towels off the rinky-dink towel rack and did my best to cover myself up. I thought it was too soon for Miss Paradise to be back with something to wear. But, I didn't worry too much about who was at the door. Shit, I'm Jason mothafuck'n Voorheeze! And I'm always ready to give anybody whatever the fuck they're looking for at any time they come looking for it. I wasn't saying that earlier when I got jacked though!

I opened the door dripping wet, with damn near the whole left side of my body exposed. Miss Paradise stood there rocking from side to side with a huge smile on her face and a bag in her hands.

I stepped aside and let her enter the room. She looked at me like I was one of them Chippendale dancers as she walked past me.

"Honey, I told you mama was going to hook you up! Now, Miss Paradise got something I just know your fine, dark, sexy ass is gone like," she said excitedly as she invited herself to take a seat on the bed.

She went inside the first bag and started pulling some pants out. "Now, these is what all the little tenders out hustling are wearing now days. They call this brand Iceberg."

The pants were a shiny color. I had never seen material like it before, but they were dope as fuck! She pulled out a pack of Hanes boxers and sat them on the bed. I didn't even think about what I was doing, I just did it. I dropped the so-called towel and walked over to the bed and picked up the pack of boxers.

"Well, I'd be damn, nephew! That big ole thang you got right there will make a bitch pay you for a date." Her eyes were half-closed while she said that after she bit her bottom lip.

"Paradise, if I didn't already have my queen, you and I would have more fun than the law would allow. Shit, I'd probably would've made a wife out of your fine ass. But as it stands, lil mama, I got respect my queen." Hopefully, the way I just shot her down was smooth enough that she would focus on the compliment and not the letdown.

"Hmmph. Well, I hope that heifer knows that she's one lucky girl." She reached back into the bag and pulled out the flyest shirt I'd ever seen. It was a flagpole gray, button-down, baseball jersey with damn near every Looney Tunes character on it. If you looked at the jersey closely, you could see faint blue pinstripes going down it. Looney Tunes was written across the shoulder blades. The shit was dope.

The last thing she pulled out the bag were a pair of throwback, bone-white 90's Air Max's. What fucked me up was the fact that everything still had the tags on them. I don't know how this thick ass dope fiend pulled it off, but she did. She'd managed to get me a whole brand spanking new outfit.

"Now, this is exactly what the fuck I'm talking about." I gave her the rest of the sack I had for Red, which was almost a two-hundred-dollar count.

Still, I counted out fifty in cash and gave it to her, after making her promise she would be back the next day with some more clothes.

Paradise grabbed her payment out of my hand. She held onto my hand when she did and asked if I was sure I didn't want to party. When I declined, she tucked everything I gave her away, minus one rock.

I let her smoke that rock in peace. When she was done, I let her out of the room and into the night. I went to put the clothes away and noticed something else was still inside one of the bags. I found a thing of brand-new sheets. I couldn't help but smile. I thought she got these because she just counted on me giving in to her temptation, until I pulled the sheets out of the bag and a note fell out. I picked it up and read it. "It would've been fun!" It had a smiley face on it.

That was the only thing written on the paper. I knew then Miss Paradise was really a sweet lady. This made me feel good, that I'd taken care of her good.

After taking the old sheets off and putting the new ones on, I kicked the comforter on the floor. I hung my clothes up in the closet and climbed in bed. Tomorrow, I had a lot of shit to do.

De'Kari

CHAPTER 17

On the 22 El Camino Real, I thought about what I needed to do. I used the ride to Palo Alto to analyze and re-analyze my game plan.

One thing for sure was I wasn't about to take no more losses. Fuck that shit! By any means, I was ready to get it in!

I followed my now-normal routine and met B.A. at the gas station. I wasn't in the mood for any small talk, so I handled my business, picked up three more ounces and asked my big cousin who I could buy a cannon (gun) from.

A person would think by now, I really couldn't be shocked. Shiiiiit! When he told me who I should talk to about the hand cannon, it seriously fucked me up.

B.A. pulled his cell phone out and called the nigga as if to assure me he wasn't bullshitting. A couple of minutes later, we were pulling up to a two-story red house on Tulane Avenue. This was the same house where my little brother Meechie lived.

When we pulled up to the house, he pulled his cell phone out again and made a call. Before he hung up his phone, my lil cousin Tut-Tut was walking out of the house.

"Handle yo business, cousin. I'm going to bend a corner or two and I'll be back to swoop you up," B.A. told me as he lit one of the many pre-rolled blunts he had.

"Off top. Good looking out, Rogue." I gave him a dap before getting out of the Camaro.

As an afterthought, he called out, "Tell Tut to hit me when y'all done."

I got out of the Camaro and met my cousin at the gate. He was smiling ear to ear.

"I told you I was BTA, dad. I might be young, but believe me, I'm with all the activities. Tell me, cousin, what are you looking for, dad?" I swear, I couldn't believe that the little nigga was only fifteen.

Thinking back on it now, when I was fifteen, I was young, dumb, reckless and a mothafuck'n problem.

I thought about what he asked. "I don't know, lil cousin, what do you got?" As a response, he told me we needed to bend a corner.

There was a two-tone blue and baby blue, two-door, Chevy Caprice sitting there. It belonged to Bubbie, Meechie's uncle. We headed to the 2500 block of Fordham and pulled up to Jack Farrell Park. Tut-Tut pulled up on the passenger side of a midnight blue, Scooby Doo van on twenty-six-inch chrome rims.

When we climbed inside, this young Puerto Rican kid was sitting in the driver's seat. Tut-Tut made the introduction once we were all in the van. Turns out, the stocky little Puerto Rican kid was called Weez.

"Tut, what's up, Rogue? You already know where everything at nigga, so do what you do, nigga," Weez told him before giving his attention back to his phone.

I watched as Tut-Tut touched a couple of things, then pushed a couple buttons on the DVD player. Moments later, I saw some real James Bond shit. The side panel of one of the walls made a hissing sound, then the entire panel slid backwards.

These two little mothafuckas had a mini arsenal. I mean, I know Village niggaz sometimes refer to their hood as Baby Vietnam, but God damn!

Tut-Tut saw the look on my face and laughed. "BTA dad, I told you my niggaz and I were 'bout that action,' ready for whatever."

"Rogue, all I got to spend is a thousand. Just tell me what you got in that range. I know niggaz who sell guns be having all kinds of off the wall prices." I mean, literally, these two niggaz had damn near every handgun imaginable on that wall. Not to mention, the machine guns at the bottom.

They both laughed at what I said. "Naaw, dad. We don't sell guns. This is our own personal shit, dad. We ain't selling you shit. Cuzzo said you needed some heat. Since you're family, me and my nigga making sure you're straight." The two looked at each other, then Tut said, "Believe me dad, we know how ugly it is out here in these streets."

I never was a fronting ass nigga, so I told him I didn't really know what half of the mothafuckas on the wall were. In response, he named off all of them.

There were two XD 40's, a 191145 with a thirty-five-round drum, three FN 57's, two Glock 23's, a Glock 26, four Glock 27's, and Glock 30's. One Ruger P85, a P-90 and a P-91, a Smith and Wesson 9mm and a Calico with a fifty-round clip, a M-16, Chinese AK and a Russian AK.

I didn't know who these two little mothafuckas had problems with, but I sure as fuck was glad it wasn't me!

When Tut-Tut was done naming everything, the nigga Weez took his attention off of his phone and told me, "Personally, Big Homie, I'd take the Glock 23. It's a 40-cal and we got a twenty-two and a thirty-stick for it. But since Mimi just told me she gone be busy tonight. We can close the panel, ride down the freeway, and take care of whatever little problem you got right now, Rogue."

After seeing their arsenal, these mothafuckas were no longer kids in my eyes. They had enough guns to protect God. I definitely believed he meant every word he said in regard to that BTA shit.

"Good looking, Rogue. It ain't like that though. A nigga just want to make sure I stay ready, so I don't have to get ready. A nigga kicked the door in to my motel room while I was out getting it. I'm just trying to make sure I don't take no more losses."

Disappointment flashed in the young wolf's eyes. I could see in those disappointed eyes that he was both willing and ready and wasn't going to do no hesitating.

I ended up taking Weez's advice, grabbing the Glock 23 with the twenty-two clip. Then I had Tut-Tut call B.A. The three of us continued to talk until he got there. I really liked both of the little niggaz. Right then and there, I decided once T'Rida and I did our thang, I was coming for both of these little niggaz and was putting them on the team.

Two and a half hours later, I was in my new room with Edwina and Q. After grabbing the cannon, B.A. dropped me back off at the Chevron. I took the clip out of the Glock and stuffed both in my pants.

The entire walk to the bus/train station, I was more scared than a snitch at a gangsta's party. On the way to the room, I stopped off at Safeway and picked up some more razors, bags and chicken. I got a page from Edwina while I was in the store. When I called, she wanted to know why I hadn't hit them up. I just told her to meet me at the room.

The there of us all met up at the motel at the same time. When I walked inside the office the young, Arab looking manager smiled at me like I was a porn star. I told him I wanted to switch to one of his best rooms and pay for the full week. He winked at me and gave me the keys. I added an extra hundred for him and asked him to order a pizza and some sodas for the ladies and have it delivered to the room.

The new room was a hell of a lot cleaner. Since all I had was the outfit on my back, I didn't need anything out of the room.

Inside the new room, the three of us got down to business. I wanted all three ounces chopped, bagged and ready to roll.

A nigga needed to make up for the shit last night. I was damn near broke again!

I had just finished cutting the first ounce when we heard a car horn honk. Figuring it was the pizza man, I stood up. I wasn't going to be nobody's fool twice, so I pulled out the Glock and the clip, slapped the mothafucka in and cocked it.

After tucking the cannon back in my waistline, I opened the door and stepped out. The older pizza guy looked terrified at the sight of the cannon on my waistline, until I pulled out my cash. As I was paying him, another car pulled up catching our attention. It was dark by now, which really made it impossible to see inside the tinted windows.

The passenger door opened, and my left hand dropped to my waist.

"Nephew! Hey, it's auntie Paradise!" she called out, seconds before that cannon came out.

I finished paying the pizza guy and sent him on his way. Paradise came sashaying up to me with a bunch of bags in her hands.

"Damn, nephew! This is my third time coming back over here. If you wasn't here this time, I was going to say fuck it, and take this shit over to my homegirl Nancy. Her old man is about your size and Nancy treat a girl as good as you do," she said as she stepped in front of me.

"Who's in the car?" I completely ignored her comment. I was on my safety and security shit.

"Aww, that's just my old man John, baby, don't worry about him."

"Well, Paradise, I'm very paranoid lil mama, so why don't you tell John to roll the window down some, so I don't fill that bitch up with a bunch of missiles." Maybe it was something in my voice, cause she spun around on her heels fast and walked to the car.

She was wearing a black, Baby Phat halter top and some sheer nylon white leggings. I guess I'm a real dirt bag, because the way her ass cheeks were jumping up and down, I could tell she didn't have any panties on. Shit, if Edwina and Q wasn't in the room, I for sure would've fell victim to lust and took her in that room and blew her back out.

John rolled the passenger front and back windows down to ease my suspicions. Paradise came back over and followed me into the room.

There was no need for introductions, so I didn't make any. Q and Edwina sat at the table in their bra and panties wrapping the rocks that I cut up, minding their business. The most attention they gave us was to look at us as we entered the room.

I looked through the bags that Paradise brought. I saw a total of eight outfits and three pair of Nike's. The outfits were all Iceberg, which was the hottest shit out. I had done a little research on the name. I'm talking a hundred dollars just for the t-shirt and up to one-fifty for the pants. The shoes were two pairs of Air Max's and one pair of Nike Foamposite's.

The average nigga would've tried to play her, cause she was a smoker, but I'm not the average nigga. Last night, she put me in the game when she brought me the fit I had on now. It was my turn to put her in the game.

One good deed deserves another.

I walked over to the table and grabbed twenty-five unwrapped rocks, a five-hundred-dollar count and put them in a sandwich bag. Next, I peeled off three hundred in cash and handed them both to her. I thought about it and retrieved ten more rocks.

She was juiced like fuck when I gave it to her. I mean, Paradise was so excited, she hugged me and kissed me on the cheeks. Her hardened nipples poked into my chest. Then, I walked her outside and to the car where John was patiently waiting. Once again, watching her massive ass jiggle and jump as she walked in front of me, I thought, *I have to be a dirtbag*, because my dick got hard as fuck.

The moment I walked back inside the room; Q got at me. "Nigga, let me find out you're over here fucking Big Booty Paradise!" She looked over at Edwina and told her, "Bitch, that really would be a low-key scrimmage."

The two of them burst out into laughter. They had waited for me to finish my business with Paradise before taking a break and eating. Now they were both sprawled across the bed with the open pizza box between them.

I put the cannon on top of the table and started putting the clothes I'd just gotten in the closet.

"Brother, what's up with the banger?" Edwina asked in between bites. Before answering, I sat down on the bed with my chicken.

While we ate our food, I told them about everything that transpired last night. In between bites of fried chicken and telling them what happened, I couldn't keep my eyes off of Q laying across the bed in her bra and panties. I still wouldn't go against my guns or my morals, so I wouldn't fuck with her.

That didn't mean a nigga couldn't get his gaze on.

She saw me looking and licked her lips. God damn, those lips were looking good, with that shiny ass gloss that she puts on them mothafuckas and the grease from the pepperoni.

"Oh, hell no. Y'all are not going to be doing no freaking and shit with me in here." My sister's words brought me out of my lustful thoughts.

I said, fuck the warmth of the room, grabbed the rest of my chicken and ate the rest of it out in the cold. I didn't need any distractions. The cold night air cleared my mind and drove the lust away.

When I walked back into the room, we finished handling our business, cutting the dope and bagging it. Once that was finished, I gave them the bed and took the floor with the cannon next to my head.

**** N. D. ****

CHAPTER 18

The following morning set the tone for our week. We bled the block, like bloodthirsty leeches attached to a healthy hippo. The three of us hooked up with Red and set downtown on fire.

We were on a mission to sell five hundred and fifty-six plastic-wrapped crack rocks, in one day. We accomplished that in just two hours. I swear to God! Downtown San Jose was like a "crack super terminal". This was *Sugar Hill* and I was Romello. I made eleven hundred, one hundred and twenty dollars in just two hours. That was a long way from making three cents per hour inside of the prison kitchen!

I told my three workers it would take me two hours to go to East Palo Alto and back there, we would spend almost two hours sacking up the rocks. No one liked that, because that was four hours we would miss hosting.

Red came up with another idea. He told me about a Pisa (Mexican National) he knew that sold powder coke to him for three hundred an ounce. That shit was unbelievable, but even if it was true, I didn't know how to cook dope. He assured me of three things.

It was surely real, the guy could meet us at his apartment down the way, and Red would cook the dope right and we would save half the time.

Life was about taking risks. The bigger the risk, the greater the reward. I was looking for a big reward, so I took the risk. On our way to Red's apartment, we stopped at Muchos, a little eatery off of Santa Clara Street, in between 2nd and 3rd. I treated everybody to lunch, which we took to his place.

The food smelled so damn good, I kept picking at my shit before we reached his spot.

I was expecting to find a rundown, filthy apartment with no furniture. I was shocked way beyond words when we walked into a clean, nicely furnished apartment. The girls couldn't help but to shower him with many compliments on his place.

While we ate, Red placed the call to his peoples, who told Red he would be at the apartment in under twenty minutes. Which he did. Out of respect for the guilty, I'll call him the connect, looked like your average Pisa. Medium height, dark hair and skin, and pudgy. His prices weren't like the average Pisa's though. When he confirmed the same price Red told me, I inquired about a half a kilo. The price was so cheap, I had to check for the whole bird.

When he told me, I almost shitted.

The shit had to be a scam. The little man assured me it wasn't. There was no need to look around and see if anyone else thought he was full of shit, because no one else was there. I sent the ladies to the store when he arrived, so we could handle business.

When I showed him I was serious about my money, he placed a call and moments later, a knock came to the door. The weight of the Glock on my waistline eased my thoughts about getting jacked. Even still, I slid it off my hip. Better safe than sorry.

The door opened and I'll be damned if the chick that walked through the door wasn't Jennifer Lopez herself. Fuck a lookalike. This was for sure, a double. I didn't pick my mouth up until after she had given him a package and walked right back out, without saying a word.

The connect showed me the bird. I cut a hole inside of it and dumped a little on Red's table. I took a small snort and instantly, my face was numb. I farted on accident and the connect laughed.

"It is primo, my friend. The purest coca in the States," he bragged.

I handed him his ninety-five hundred and assured him this was the beginning of a very beautiful thing. He left and we waited on the girls to get back. We didn't have to wait too long. When they came back, we turned Red's apartment into a subdivision for Betty Crocker's. I watched as Red cooked up a nine-piece (nine ounces).

He wanted to bring back double, (eighteen ounces,) but I told him to only put in four ounces of the baking soda the girls went and bought. Now it's true, I would be shorting myself out of two ounces. But the dope would be so good, it would be the only thing they would buy.

In the kitchen, away from the girls, I gave him an ounce for himself. I also told him when we were done, I'd give him another one, soft (powder instead of crack).

I cut the ounces up while they bagged them up. The girls did it in their bra and panties again. Red was cool peoples, but he still was a smoker, so I had him strip to his boxers. Being the "G" that I am, I wasn't trying to play him, so I stripped down to mine as well.

We were back on the block an hour later, with enough dope to last. All night, we got our grind on. By the time we quit, everyone was beat. We were all excited though. We'd made more than double what we had made earlier.

We all stayed the night at Red's apartment. While the girls slept, he and I cooked, cut, and bagged. While he got high in between day and night for three days, we followed this routine. That's how long it took to sell the entire kilo, rock for rock.

Along the way, I'd sold a filthy fifty-dollar double-up here and there. A couple thirty-dollar, sixty-dollar double-ups and a quarter ounce or two to a few of the hustlers. I'm not going to sit and go through all of the math over how much a night made. I leave that up to you all. My readers. I'll just say I was on like shit.

The girls both had fifteen thousand a piece on them. They could not have been happier. The three of us left Red alone with some fine ass redbone he called over to party with him.

I had a pocket full of money, two bad bitches on my side and a big ass ugly something on my hip. If a nigga had to ask himself what was wrong with this picture, it's because he was a fucking fool.

Since I wasn't a fool, I had the girls show me where the car dealerships were at. It was a nice and warm, sunny Bay Area day. The temperature was in the eighties in San Jose and nothing could be better.

Our minds were set before we actually got there, as far as how long the process would take before we were actually riding off in the sunset. All of that shit went out of the window the moment we walked onto the lot of Quincy Norton's Cars and Trucks. It was a used car lot that had a lot of fly shit. A bunch of Lexus's, one or two Beamers, one Vet, a few Benz. When I say fly shit, I mean fly shit. What caught my eye was a pearl gold, 2000 Cadillac SLS, with peanut butter leather interior, sunroof, Digital Bose audio sound. All of this was on top of Zenith tires and 100x triple gold Dayton's.

There wasn't anything to talk about, that shit was me. I walked into the office and thirty minutes later, I was driving away feeling like them two little niggaz that were blowing up on the radio rapping about being "ICY."

**** N. D. ****

"/Family roll thick like syrup and milkshakes/ transporting weight from the South to the Golden Gate/figure eight'n at

the light burning rubber is hype/ in the middle of the intersection tryna start up a sideshow/ My mind going other places cats don't speak on/ serve that raw and uncut for you niggaz to tweak on...../ Coke-white t-shirt blue jeans and Nikes/Coke-white t-shirt blue jeans and Nikes/ Staying strapped with the .45 wish a nigga would try/."

I was pushing down the freeway feeling like the nigga Keak Da Sneak. I wasn't pushing a coke-white T or blue jeans. I had on some deep blue Iceberg jeans, with the Iceberg Bugs Bunny t-shirt and fresh pair of Air Max's. I was feeling a fresh like that nigga times two.

I'd just left Lozano's Hand Car Wash in Mountain View. The Caddy had a fresh wax job and was gleaming. After dropping the girls off the other day, I decided to see my Lil Mama, so she could see how a real nigga put it down. When the caddy pulled up in front of 3951 66th Avenue, everybody was looking.

I dicked her down with some of that "make the neighbors call the police" sex and then told her we were going to tear down the mall. I'm not even going to lie, she looked at me like I told her the pussy was sour. Maybe she thought I was talking about shopping with her money, I don't know.

I was too busy watching the look on her face when she saw me disarm the alarm on the Caddy. I further fucked her up when I told her, "Here, Lil Mama, you drive while a nigga relax a bit."

"La'Mont, I'm not driving that! I don't know whose car you stole. But you shouldn't have it parked out in front of my apartments so some thugs could come and shoot up my house!"

I laughed so hard I nearly had a heart attack!

No matter what I said, I couldn't convince her the car was mine. She didn't calm down until I showed her the paperwork to the vehicle. That got her little ass to move.

We started at the Hilltop Mall in Richmond, then Southland Mall in Hayward, Newpark Mall in Newark, The Great Mall of the Bay Area in Milpitas and we finished our five-city spree at the Valley Fair Mall in San Jose.

After shopping, we had a little dinner at The Cheesecake Factory!

This is why I was in such a good mood as I exited Highway 280 on Page Mill, heading towards East Palo Alto. Keak Da Sneak and E-40 had me feeling myself. Especially the part of being strapped with the .45.

"/Coke white T-shirt blue jeans and Nikes, Coke white t-shirt blue jeans and Nikes/Coke white t-shirt blue jeans and Nikes, stay strapped with the .45 I wish a nigga try/"

I wasn't taking my chances driving through Palo Alto, because I knew how the police were. I thought about pulling over and letting Lil Mama drive but shrugged it off. I was doing fifty-five miles per hour and the music wasn't loud. I was cool.

The moment I saw the red and blue lights in the rear view, I regretted my decision about her driving.

"Fuck!"

She looked over at me. "Baby, what's wrong?"

"The police is behind us. Look open the glove box and press the trunk button." The moment she did, the passenger front six by nine box swung open.

She looked like a ghost fell in her lap.

"Reach inside of there and grab that plastic bag. Hurry." I had ten thousand wrapped in plastic inside every speaker housing in the car.

She pulled the Ziploc bag out like I told her and placed it in her purse. I felt bad when her eyes got as big as saucers the moment I pulled the Glock .23 off of my waistband, but I didn't have any time to talk. Except to tell her to put them in the hole.

Seconds later, I was pulling over. Right in front of a school. Just being Black and getting pulled over was enough reason to be scared. Yet, I was having too good of a day to be fucked up by anyone. Even the police.

"What seems to be the problem, sir?" I was cool as Alaska.

"Do you have any idea how fast you were going?" The way he asked me seemed innocent enough.

"Yes, sir. I was doing fifty-five miles per hour. Exactly the speed limit," I replied.

He stepped back smiling and looked across the street at the school. He didn't have to speak. I know what he was saying.

"Well, sir. I've been driving this route for years. I'll admit it has been some time since I've driven. I don't ever recall a school being on this street. Had I known I would've slowed down."

"Um-hmp! License and registration please," was all he said.

I grabbed my driver's permit and reached inside the glove box for the registration. When he asked me if I was on probation or parole, I told him yes as I handed him my registration.

"You don't have anything illegal in the car, do you, son?"

"No, sir." I said this will pure false confidence.

**** N. D. ****

De'Kari

CHAPTER 19

The false confidence decimated when he walked back to the window and told me my license was suspended. Even after telling him that had to be a mistake because I'd just gotten my permit the day before, he still wasn't listening. He told me the date of the offense that suspended the license and I told him I was in Pelican Bay at the time. He still didn't give a fuck. That actually made shit worse.

Man, it only got worse. Although he could've issued a ticket and let Lil Mama drive the car, this asshole decided to tow my shit. It was the most embarrassing shit ever. We sat on the side of the road with damn near twenty different bags. Waiting on a freaking taxicab.

I could tell Little Mama was both scared and embarrassed throughout the whole ordeal. I was thankful she listened and grabbed the dough out the door.

Once the cops left, I counted off five G's from the money and instructed her to keep the rest with her. When the cab driver pulled up, she gave him a G up front and instructed him to take us to East Oakland.

My mood continued to worsen through the hoops and hassles with the Stanford Police Department and the tow company that had my shit. I was on the phone dealing with their bullshit for hours.

I ended up having to agree to give the police department five hundred dollars in order to get them to agree to signing the release form.

Lil Mama did her best to take my mind off of the stress with some good loving, but it didn't work. Shit felt good as fuck, but it didn't work.

The following day, I spent two and a half hours at the police station, even after giving them the money. My temperature was about fifty degrees higher than the eighty-two it was outside.

The fat sweaty redneck white boy with the sergeant stripes on his uniform, easily read my growing irritation. The stupid, "fuck boi" look on his face was proof of that. Finally, they gave me the release and Lil Mama drove me from the police station to the tow yard.

Lil Mama and I made the trip over to the yard in complete silence. The only thing on my mind was all the money I had stashed in the car. We're talking over a hundred racks, which was the money I made from selling the kilo, rock for rock.

The nigga at the tow yard started to give me some shit about getting my shit out the impound. The signed release form from the police and the look on my face put an end to all of the bullshit. Every now and then, Little Mama would squeeze my hand reassuringly to remind me to keep my cool.

I'm not going to lie. I just wanted my money. I grinded hard for that shit.

Finally, they brought me my shit and I could tell right away something was wrong. Call it intuition or whatever you want to call it. I just knew something was wrong.

I popped the glove box and pushed the button for the trunk. Nothing happened. I pushed the button a second time. The results were the exact same, the speaker was jammed.

When I walked over to the passenger side of the car and manually pulled the speaker open, I noticed the Glock wasn't inside the compartment.

I walked to the back of the Caddy, popped the trunk and checked the inside of the speaker box of one my 15's speakers. There was supposed to be twenty-five thousand inside of it.

The shit was empty. I didn't have to see the steam rising from my forehead. I could feel it as my patience evaporated.

I walked back into the office like I was back on a penitentiary, Level 4 yard.

Lil Mama saw the look on my face, a look she has seen numerous times before.

"La'Mont, baby..." she tried.

I didn't give her the chance to finish whatever she thought she was going to say. I held my hand up, silencing her.

"Lil Mama, go wait for me outside. I'll be out in a moment. She wanted to protest further. The sternness inside of my voice left no room for debate.

The white boy looked to be in his forties. His balding head, protruding stomach and bulbous nose, added about ten to fifteen years on his appearance, making him look to be in his fifties.

The smug look on his face reassured me that he knew exactly what was on my mind.

"Is there a problem with your car, Mr. Simpson?" he smirked feigning to look innocent.

I walked right up to the counter and read his name tag. Then looked him square in his eyes.

"Listen good, Nick, cause I'm not about to play games with you, or nobody else about my shit. Since you found everything, you should already know I don't play games. I want my shit! All of my shit! And I want it now!" My voice was low and venomous. It resembled an angry growl.

"Well, look here, boy. Now, I don't know what you're talking about. Neither me nor none of my boys removed anything from your vehicle. But listen here. I tell you, boy, if for some reason you had something illegal inside of your vehicle, you should be glad the authorities didn't find it and give you some charges. And have your little black ass sitting in some jail over yonder." He actually smiled at me as he said it.

"Cracker, I'm not about to play with you. I don't give a fuck about the police or any of that bullshit you're talking. Either give me my shit, or we can get on some gangsta shit!" An arguing contest was the last thing I was about to get into

He reached under his counter and reached for something. I was contemplating going upside his fucking head. When his hand came back into view, he was holding my Glock 23 in his hand.

"Now, look-it here, you fucking nigger bitch! I advise you and your nigger cunt to get your black asses off of my fucking lot, before I get off into some gangster shit." His face was cherry red, and his nose was flared.

In my mind, I could see him pulling the trigger and concocting some bullshit ass story as to why he killed me.

I simply smiled at him like he was my next-door neighbor and said, "Say less," meaning there wasn't anything to talk about.

I slowly backed away, careful not to make any sudden movements that would cause this mothafucka to get happy with that trigger. I didn't dare turn my back on him either. I backed all the way into the closed door.

That's when I slowly turned around. I opened the door, wishing this mothafucka would call me back. I truly, from the bottom of my heart, didn't want no problems. But the cards had been dealt and my hands were pushed.

"Baby, please. Whatever it is, God will fix it, La'Mont. Please just let it go." Lil Mama came rushing into my arms the moment I was outside.

I tried to pull her off me, but she wouldn't break her hold. She held on like her life depended on it.

"Lil Mama, it's okay. Get in the car, baby. I got some shit that I got to take care of. It'll be okay," I whispered soothingly into her ear.

The gentleness in which I spoke was a complete contrast to the raging fire burning inside of me. After a little more coaxing, I was finally able to convince her to drive home. I had some gangsta shit to get into!

**** N. D. ****

The "Scooby Doo" van was parked exactly where it had been before. Weez was in the van smoking a blunt when I pulled up. A dope fiend was just walking away after being served his issue of dope.

Although I felt like a complete jackass, I told the young killer everything that had transpired. I didn't leave out not one tidbit of information. When I was done talking, he simply reached in his pocket for his Motorola two-way and punched some shit in.

After he was done typing, he looked up at me. "Shit nigga, you bubbled up to a key and flipped that bitch, all in the time since I saw you. Nigga, after we take care of this for you, you got to put a nigga on down there where you eating at."

I didn't have a problem with that. There was enough down in San Jose for all of us.

Tut-Tut came rolling up on a BMX Mongoose, smiling like he already knew he was going to win the lotto. "Let's get it in, dad," he said as he climbed off the bike.

Little cousin climbed up in the van like we were getting ready to go to Great America Theme Park. Weez pulled off, while Tut-Tut did his little secret touching, causing the side panel to slide open.

Tut-Tut grabbed the all-black Mack-10 with the thirty-stick. I grabbed two of the FN 57's, both of them holding thirty. When the van stopped, Weez climbed in the back. His entire demeanor was different.

"Let's show these mothafuck'n white boys how E.P.A. niggaz move." Weez's voice was titanium cold when he spoke.

Removing the M-16 off the rack, Weez looked to be right at home in his element. We climbed out of the Scooby Doo van and piled into a silver four-door Chrysler New Yorker. Because I was the one who knew where the tow yard was, I was the driver. We drove in silence. Each one of us lost in his own thoughts.

Twenty minutes later, we were parked a little ways down from the yard. Thoughts of getting my money back more vivid now than earlier. From our vantage point, we could see almost all of the lights on at the yard. There were at least three or four people inside that I could tell.

"What you think, dad?" Tut-Tut asked Weez.

"Shit Blood, I think MiMi cooked some fried chicken tonight. I ain't got time to be sitting in a parked stolo, talking to you two mothafuckas about what we should be doing." With that, he opened the door and stepped out of the New Yorker like we were in Desert Storm stepping out of a Humvee.

I would've rather had a plan but fuck it, it was time to get it in!

When we opened the door, a little rinky-dink bell rattled off alerting whoever was inside of our presence. Wasn't long before the door to the back left of the office opened.

Taat! Taat! Taat! Taat! Taat!

Weez didn't hesitate to make the mothafucka who opened the door do the Harlem Shake as he filled his body with 223's. The back door to the office was snatched open.

"Hey, Nick! Are you?" The question was cut short by the hail of forty-five bullets from Tut-Tut's Mack-10.

Taat! Taat! Taat! Taat! Taat! Taat! Taat!

The cocksucker was blown back out of the door he had just came through. I followed close behind his dead body, stepping over it as I made my way into the yard.

Boca! Boca!

I dropped to my knee and scanned the darkness where the shots came from.

"You fucking niggers better git your ass out of here!" came from the darkness to my left.

"Where's my shit, white boy?" I called out. Weez and Tut-Tut both filed out of the office on the opposite side of me.

"Don't know! Don't fucking care Spook! Nick and John's the ones took your shit and the both of them dead, so there! You fucking niggers better geeet before the boys come, I tell ya." All that talking gave us a precise location of his hiding place.

"In that case…" was all Weez said before he lit the night up like a firework display.

Taat! Taat! Taat! Taat! Tut-Tut followed Weez's lead. Just like that, any answer as to where my money was died right along with them white boys.

My soul shattered as sparks flew from bullets ricocheting off the metal of parked cars. I never let off one single shot from the FN's.

We made our way back to the New Yorker like nothing happened.

"Hey what's all the noise?"

Bocca! Bocca! Bocca!

I spun to my right and let one of the FN's respond to the question the innocent bystander asked. These two little motha-fuckas were out of their minds if they thought I wouldn't let my shit speak for me.

For the most part, we rode back in silence. My mind was in a state of shock over losing my money for a second time.

Some would say I was crying over spilled milk. Maybe, but those are the same mothafuckas that have never touched that much money before.

"Shit, dad. That's our bad about your money, dad. Niggaz was only thinking about riding on them fools. That's what we do, dad. We ride on mothafuckas, all the way BTA, dad." I guess that was Tut-Tut's way of cheering me up.

"It's good, Rogue. That's just a big pill to swallow." I was trying my best to swallow it though.

"Rogue, if a nigga know like I know, there's only two things in life that's given. One, a nigga is gone take losses. Second, niggaz always gonna war. A young nigga like me don't count the losses, cause I'm built for this war shit." Weez paused for a second, then added, "War and MiMi's fried chicken." We all laughed at that.

We ditched the stolo and made our back to Jack Farrell Park. We all went our separate ways. Before separating, Tut-Tut assured me that he had a for-sure way to get rid of the guns. Family or not, I wasn't trusting anybody enough to do that.

I told him I would take care of the FN myself. Then I jumped on the freeway, headed to Lil Mama's place.

True shit! I told her about the money and cried myself to sleep in her arms. I didn't tell her about what we had did.

****N.D.****

CHAPTER 20

I got up nice and early to make sure I had enough time to catch the 5:00 a.m. to see what they reported about last night. I stayed on my "safety and security" shit like that.

It turned out the tow yard was a hub-station for methamphetamine ring that the Hells Angels was running. Police claim they found fifty pounds of pure meth, along with three hundred thousand in cash and some guns in the front office. I felt sick to my stomach. All of that shit was only a few away from us.

Fucking story of my life.

I was that close to making sure my brother T'Rida came home to something nice. As it is, my nigga came home yesterday and all I got is a bunch of excuses and war stories. Neither one was worth the time they took to be told.

"Babe. Did you get that number I asked for?" I asked Lil Mama when I walked back into the room.

"Mmmm. Yeah, it's over on the dresser next to the jewelry box," she called back, still asleep.

I walked over to the dresser and picked the paper up. Walking next to the house phone, I went into the living room and made the call.

She picked up on the third ring. "Hello?"

"Moe Money! What's up, little sis?" I yelled into the phone.

"Jason?" she asked.

"Boy do you know what time it is?"

"The one and only. Moe, you know I had to let you do your honeymoon thing yesterday, but now I need to holla at my big brother regardless of what time it is, big sis." Damn, it was going to feel good to hear my niggaz voice after all this time.

I heard Monique telling him it was me on the phone.

"V, what's hood wit it, Cuzzo?" My mothafuck'n big brother came over the phone.

"T-Mothafuck'n Rida! Welcome home, my nigga, I thought niggaz woke up early on the yard, mothafucka?" I joked into the phone once I heard T'Rida's voice.

"This ain't da pen, cousin. And how you get dis number anyway, nigga?" Here he go with all that *Secret Squirrel* shit. How God ain't supposed to have his house phone number?

"Come on, Rogue, you know how I fucks wit it. So why you got' ask me some dumb ass shit like that?" I had to laugh at that before continuing. "I got a couple of connections, down at the phone company."

"Yeah, I heard that, nigga. The president ain't supposed to have this number. Anyway, what's hood wit it though?" T'Rida spoke into the phone.

"Rogue, I got some shit to take care of yo way. When a nigga done, I'mma swing by yo spot. I should be sliding through in like three hours," I told him just before hanging up the phone.

I woke Lil Mama up after I got off the phone. She wanted me to go with her to the gym and show her a few workout routines. She'd just gotten a monthly membership and she swore if I helped her, she would stick with it.

A few hours later, I had her drop me off on Sundale, the street that Monique and T'Rida lived on. I made my way to the door loving the early morning chill. After knocking on the door, I waited for my nigga to open the door.

When he looked in the peephole, I wrote it off to one of the security flaws that came along with being away from the streets so long. Niggaz don't look through peepholes. That's how you get your shit knocked off.

T'Rida swung the door wide open and had a huge, shit-eating grin on his face.

We embraced like long lost Army buddies.

"Brah, you want a drink?" T'Rida asked once we broke our embrace.

"Nigga, do a bear shit in the woods and wipe his ass with a rabbit?" Fuck did he mean, did I want a drink?

"There you go with all them riddles and shit," T'Rida shot back.

"Yeah nigga, you know I want someth'n to sip on."

T'Rida turned to pour me a drink. When he turned back to hand it to me, he told me, "On some real shit, V! Nigga, we gotta eat, my nigga. I can't do this small shit no more, brah."

"Rogue, you ain't saying noth'n the kid ain't been thinking himself. A nigga so hungry, I'll eat a bowl of soup wit a fork around dis bitch." I was so for real about this shit.

"My nigga, I've been thinking about shit and dis here ain't da business," T'Rida told me in a voice full of sincerity and desperation.

I sat and listened as T'Rida laid out an idea that he'd been mauling over in his head for a little while. I was liking the shit I was hearing, but we were going to need more than my two FN's.

I thought about Tut-Tut and Weez. Before I could mention them, T'Rida brought up a name that would be perfect. Lenard "Tommy Gunz" Walker.

We couldn't go wrong with Tommy Gunz by our side. After all, the shit T'Rida was talking about doing was some *Behind Enemy Lines* type of shit and having a loose cannon with brains was just the doctor ordered.

While we talked, Monique whipped up some breakfast that smelled like I would kill ten niggaz, just to get a taste of it. Moe made enough food for all of us and fa'sho, I got my grub on. T'Rida continued to go over his game plan.

After eating breakfast, T'Rida and I hopped in Monique's bucket on our way to East Oakland. We were two young hungry wolves, listening to Messy Marv's *Turf Politics* on a journey to meet that thick bad bitch called Destiny. Either we were going to make it happen, or we were going to tangle with the Devil.

One thing was certain though, fuck getting rich or die trying. This wasn't a movie. It was real life and niggaz were playing for keeps. We weren't taking no loses.

It was Neva Die or Nothing!
Long Live the will to win!
276!

Submission Guideline

Submit the first three chapters of your completed manuscript to ldpsubmissions@gmail.com, subject line: Your book's title. The manuscript must be in a .doc file and sent as an attachment. Document should be in Times New Roman, double spaced and in size 12 font. Also, provide your synopsis and full contact information. If sending multiple submissions, they must each be in a separate email.

Have a story but no way to send it electronically? You can still submit to LDP/Ca$h Presents. Send in the first three chapters, written or typed, of your completed manuscript to:

LDP: Submissions Dept
Po Box 944
Stockbridge, Ga 30281

DO NOT send original manuscript. Must be a duplicate.

Provide your synopsis and a cover letter containing your full contact information.

Thanks for considering LDP and Ca$h Presents.

BOW DOWN TO MY GANGSTA

By **Ca$h**

TORN BETWEEN TWO

By **Coffee**

THE STREETS STAINED MY SOUL **II**

By **Marcellus Allen**

BLOOD OF A BOSS **VI**

SHADOWS OF THE GAME II

By **Askari**

LOYAL TO THE GAME **IV**

By **T.J. & Jelissa**

A DOPEBOY'S PRAYER **II**

By **Eddie "Wolf" Lee**

IF LOVING YOU IS WRONG... **III**

By **Jelissa**

TRUE SAVAGE **VII**

MIDNIGHT CARTEL III

DOPE BOY MAGIC IV

By **Chris Green**

BLAST FOR ME **III**

A SAVAGE DOPEBOY III

CUTTHROAT MAFIA II

By **Ghost**

A HUSTLER'S DECEIT III

KILL ZONE **II**

BAE BELONGS TO ME III

A DOPE BOY'S QUEEN II

By **Aryanna**

CHAINED TO THE STREETS III

By **J-Blunt**

COKE KINGS V

KING OF THE TRAP II

By **T.J. Edwards**

GORILLAZ IN THE BAY V

De'Kari

THE STREETS ARE CALLING II

Duquie Wilson

KINGPIN KILLAZ IV

STREET KINGS III

PAID IN BLOOD III

CARTEL KILLAZ IV

DOPE GODS II

Hood Rich

SINS OF A HUSTLA II

ASAD

TRIGGADALE III

Elijah R. Freeman

KINGZ OF THE GAME V

Playa Ray

SLAUGHTER GANG IV

RUTHLESS HEART IV

By Willie Slaughter

THE HEART OF A SAVAGE III

By Jibril Williams

FUK SHYT II

By Blakk Diamond

THE REALEST KILLAS

By Tranay Adams

TRAP GOD II

By Troublesome

YAYO IV

A SHOOTER'S AMBITION III

By S. Allen

GHOST MOB

Stilloan Robinson

KINGPIN DREAMS III

By Paper Boi Rari

CREAM

By Yolanda Moore

SON OF A DOPE FIEND II

By Renta

FOREVER GANGSTA II

GLOCKS ON SATIN SHEETS II

By Adrian Dulan

LOYALTY AIN'T PROMISED II

By Keith Williams

THE PRICE YOU PAY FOR LOVE II

DOPE GIRL MAGIC III

By Destiny Skai

CONFESSIONS OF A GANGSTA II

By Nicholas Lock

I'M NOTHING WITHOUT HIS LOVE II

By Monet Dragun

CAUGHT UP IN THE LIFE III

By Robert Baptiste

NEW TO THE GAME III

By **Malik D. Rice**

LIFE OF A SAVAGE IV

A GANGSTA'S QUR'AN II

By **Romell Tukes**

QUIET MONEY II

By **Trai'Quan**

THE STREETS MADE ME II

By **Larry D. Wright**

THE ULTIMATE SACRIFICE VI

IF YOU CROSSM ME ONCE II

By **Anthony Fields**

THE LIFE OF A HOOD STAR

By Ca$h & Rashia Wilson

Available Now

RESTRAINING ORDER **I & II**

By **CA$H & Coffee**

LOVE KNOWS NO BOUNDARIES **I II & III**

By **Coffee**

RAISED AS A GOON I, II, III & IV

BRED BY THE SLUMS I, II, III

BLAST FOR ME I & II

ROTTEN TO THE CORE I II III

A BRONX TALE I, II, III

DUFFEL BAG CARTEL I II III IV

HEARTLESS GOON I II III IV

A SAVAGE DOPEBOY I II

HEARTLESS GOON I II III

DRUG LORDS I II III

CUTTHROAT MAFIA

By **Ghost**

LAY IT DOWN **I & II**

LAST OF A DYING BREED

BLOOD STAINS OF A SHOTTA I & II III

By **Jamaica**

LOYAL TO THE GAME I II III

LIFE OF SIN I, II III

By **TJ & Jelissa**

BLOODY COMMAS I & II

SKI MASK CARTEL I II & III

KING OF NEW YORK I II,III IV V

RISE TO POWER I II III

COKE KINGS I II III IV

BORN HEARTLESS I II III IV

KING OF THE TRAP

By **T.J. Edwards**

IF LOVING HIM IS WRONG…I & II

LOVE ME EVEN WHEN IT HURTS I II III

By **Jelissa**

WHEN THE STREETS CLAP BACK I & II III

THE HEART OF A SAVAGE I II

By **Jibril Williams**

A DISTINGUISHED THUG STOLE MY HEART I II & III

LOVE SHOULDN'T HURT I II III IV

RENEGADE BOYS I II III IV

PAID IN KARMA I II III

By **Meesha**

A GANGSTER'S CODE I &, II III

A GANGSTER'S SYN I II III

THE SAVAGE LIFE I II III

CHAINED TO THE STREETS I II

By **J-Blunt**

PUSH IT TO THE LIMIT

By **Bre' Hayes**

BLOOD OF A BOSS **I, II, III, IV, V**

SHADOWS OF THE GAME

By **Askari**

THE STREETS BLEED MURDER **I, II & III**

THE HEART OF A GANGSTA I II& III

By **Jerry Jackson**

CUM FOR ME I II III IV V

An **LDP Erotica Collaboration**

BRIDE OF A HUSTLA **I II & II**

THE FETTI GIRLS **I, II& III**

CORRUPTED BY A GANGSTA I, II III, IV

BLINDED BY HIS LOVE

THE PRICE YOU PAY FOR LOVE

DOPE GIRL MAGIC I II

By **Destiny Skai**

WHEN A GOOD GIRL GOES BAD

By **Adrienne**

THE COST OF LOYALTY I II III

By Kweli

A GANGSTER'S REVENGE **I II III & IV**

THE BOSS MAN'S DAUGHTERS I II III IV V

A SAVAGE LOVE **I & II**

BAE BELONGS TO ME I II

A HUSTLER'S DECEIT I, II, III

WHAT BAD BITCHES DO I, II, III

SOUL OF A MONSTER I II III

KILL ZONE

A DOPE BOY'S QUEEN

By **Aryanna**

A KINGPIN'S AMBITON

A KINGPIN'S AMBITION **II**

I MURDER FOR THE DOUGH

By **Ambitious**

TRUE SAVAGE I II III IV V VI

DOPE BOY MAGIC I, II, III

MIDNIGHT CARTEL I II

By **Chris Green**

A DOPEBOY'S PRAYER

By **Eddie "Wolf" Lee**

THE KING CARTEL **I, II & III**

By **Frank Gresham**

THESE NIGGAS AIN'T LOYAL **I, II & III**

By **Nikki Tee**

GANGSTA SHYT **I II &III**

By **CATO**

THE ULTIMATE BETRAYAL

By **Phoenix**

BOSS'N UP **I , II & III**

By **Royal Nicole**

I LOVE YOU TO DEATH

By Destiny J

I RIDE FOR MY HITTA

I STILL RIDE FOR MY HITTA

By **Misty Holt**

LOVE & CHASIN' PAPER

By **Qay Crockett**

TO DIE IN VAIN

SINS OF A HUSTLA

By **ASAD**

BROOKLYN HUSTLAZ

By **Boogsy Morina**

BROOKLYN ON LOCK I & II

By **Sonovia**

GANGSTA CITY

By **Teddy Duke**

A DRUG KING AND HIS DIAMOND I & II III

A DOPEMAN'S RICHES

HER MAN, MINE'S TOO I, II

CASH MONEY HO'S

By Nicole Goosby

TRAPHOUSE KING **I II & III**

KINGPIN KILLAZ I II III

STREET KINGS I II

PAID IN BLOOD **I II**

CARTEL KILLAZ I II III

DOPE GODS

By **Hood Rich**

LIPSTICK KILLAH **I, II, III**

CRIME OF PASSION I II & III

By **Mimi**

STEADY MOBBN' **I, II, III**

THE STREETS STAINED MY SOUL

By **Marcellus Allen**

WHO SHOT YA **I, II, III**

SON OF A DOPE FIEND

Renta

GORILLAZ IN THE BAY **I II III IV**

TEARS OF A GANGSTA I II

DE'KARI

TRIGGADALE I II

Elijah R. Freeman

GOD BLESS THE TRAPPERS I, II, III

THESE SCANDALOUS STREETS I, II, III

FEAR MY GANGSTA I, II, III

THESE STREETS DON'T LOVE NOBODY I, II

BURY ME A G I, II, III, IV, V

A GANGSTA'S EMPIRE I, II, III, IV

THE DOPEMAN'S BODYGAURD I II

Tranay Adams

THE STREETS ARE CALLING

Duquie Wilson

MARRIED TO A BOSS... I II III

By Destiny Skai & Chris Green

KINGZ OF THE GAME I II III IV

Playa Ray

SLAUGHTER GANG I II III

RUTHLESS HEART I II III

By Willie Slaughter

FUK SHYT

By Blakk Diamond

DON'T F#CK WITH MY HEART I II

By Linnea

ADDICTED TO THE DRAMA I II III

By Jamila

YAYO I II III

A SHOOTER'S AMBITION I II

By S. Allen

TRAP GOD

By Troublesome

FOREVER GANGSTA

GLOCKS ON SATIN SHEETS

By Adrian Dulan

TOE TAGZ I II III

By Ah'Million

KINGPIN DREAMS I II

By Paper Boi Rari

CONFESSIONS OF A GANGSTA

By Nicholas Lock

I'M NOTHING WITHOUT HIS LOVE

By Monet Dragun

CAUGHT UP IN THE LIFE I II

By Robert Baptiste

NEW TO THE GAME I II

By **Malik D. Rice**

LIFE OF A SAVAGE I II III

A GANGSTA'S QUR'AN

By **Romell Tukes**

LOYALTY AIN'T PROMISED

By Keith Williams

Quiet Money

By **Trai'Quan**

THE STREETS MADE ME
By **Larry D. Wright**
THE ULTIMATE SACRIFICE I, II, III, IV, V
KHADIFI
IF YOU CROSS ME ONCE
By **Anthony Fields**
THE LIFE OF A HOOD STAR
By **Ca$h & Rashia Wilson**

BOOKS BY LDP'S CEO, CA$H

TRUST IN NO MAN

TRUST IN NO MAN 2

TRUST IN NO MAN 3

BONDED BY BLOOD

SHORTY GOT A THUG

THUGS CRY

THUGS CRY 2

THUGS CRY 3

TRUST NO BITCH

TRUST NO BITCH 2

TRUST NO BITCH 3

TIL MY CASKET DROPS

RESTRAINING ORDER

RESTRAINING ORDER 2

IN LOVE WITH A CONVICT

LIFE OF A HOOD STAR

Coming Soon

BONDED BY BLOOD 2

BOW DOWN TO MY GANGSTA

Tears of a Gangsta 2

www.ingramcontent.com/pod-product-compliance
Lightning Source LLC
Chambersburg PA
CBHW070524260626
47161CB00004B/1631